Dear Reader

What a delight to be able to share with you the story of Lorelai and Woody. As authors, we always fall in love with our characters, and these two were no exception. Lorelai has such gumption, and I love the way she's firm but loving with headstrong three-year-old Hannah. Woody is tall and delicious—a man who loves life and is honourable in the way he lives up to high expectations.

We were fortunate enough to spend our Christmas vacation travelling through the Snowy Mountains of Australia. Even though it was during the height of the Australian summer, the weather in that part of the country changed frequently. One day we were sunburnt; the next day we had snow! It was delightfully inspiring.

We sincerely hope you enjoy reading about Lorelai and Woody, and accompanying them on their journey as together they find joy, hope and love.

Warmest regards

Lucy Clark

Lucy Clark is actually a husband-and-wife writing team. They enjoy taking holidays with their children, during which they discuss and develop new ideas for their books using the fantastic Australian scenery. They use their daily walks to talk over characterisation and fine details of the wonderful stories they produce, and are avid movie buffs. They live on the edge of a popular wine district in South Australia with their two children, and enjoy spending family time together at weekends.

TAMING THE LONE DOC'S HEART

BY
LUCY CLARK

First published in Great Britain 2012
by Mills & Boon, an imprint of Harlequin (UK) Limited.
Harlequin (UK) Limited, Eton House, 18-24 Paradise Road,
Richmond, Surrey TW9 1SR

© Anne Clark & Peter Clark 2012

ISBN: 978 0 263 22860 1

Harlequin (UK) policy is to use papers that are natural, renewable and recyclable products and made from wood grown in sustainable forests. The logging and manufacturing process conform to the legal environmental regulations of the country of origin.

Printed and bound in Great Britain
by CPI Antony Rowe, Chippenham, Wiltshire

Recent titles by the same author:

THE BOSS SHE CAN'T RESIST
WEDDING ON THE BABY WARD
SPECIAL CARE BABY MIRACLE
DOCTOR DIAMOND IN THE ROUGH
THE DOCTOR'S SOCIETY SWEETHEART
THE DOCTOR'S DOUBLE TROUBLE

These books are also available in ebook format
from www.millsandboon.co.uk

To Vikie & Luke
Congratulations on finding your happily-ever-after!

Jer 33:11

PROLOGUE

'WOODY?' Lorelai's breathing was erratic and she knew she had to control it. She gripped the phone tighter in her hand, channelling her frustration into the inanimate object.

'Lorelai? How did the meeting go?'

'There's been an accident. I need you.' She worked hard to keep the panic from her voice but knew she'd failed. She walked around to the rear of her car, which her father had parked on the shoulder closest to the mountain.

'What is it? What's happened?' There was a briskness to his words, the ever-present direct pitch of a surgeon switching his mind into 'action' mode. She'd never been more grateful that Woody had come to Oodnaminaby to visit his sister, Honey, especially as she could do with a skilled surgeon to help her.

'A car…drove through the barrier. He swerved then… just…went off the road. And…' Lorelai tried to control her wobbling voice. 'It's John.'

'John? Your husband?'

'Yes, and his *mistress* was in the car with him.' She retrieved her medical bag from the boot and slammed the lid shut. 'Dad and I were driving right behind them. We saw the whole thing. I watched him lose control and veer off, smashing through the...' Her breathing had increased and she stopped, trying to slow herself down, to be calm and composed. If she was to be of any help, she needed to find her focus.

'Lorelai? Are you OK? You and your dad? You're both all right?'

'We're fine.' Lorelai walked quickly but carefully towards the broken guard rail, wanting to see what had happened but by the same token not wanting to know. 'Dad's controlling the traffic and calling the ambulance, fire rescue and police workers, as well as ordering the heavy machinery needed.' That's it, she told herself. Focus on the overall picture. Breathe. In, out. In, out.

'Right. Good. Glad you're both safe.' There was relief in his tone and she allowed his calm, deep tone to wash over her, helping to quell the rising panic. 'Where are you?'

Lorelai gave him directions and could hear him moving about in the background, the sounds of a small baby in the distance. *Her* baby. Her beautiful little girl who John hadn't wanted. He hadn't wanted to be a father. He hadn't wanted to be married to her any more. He'd chosen to be with his mistress and he'd wanted to get a divorce. Lorelai had agreed. She'd attended the meeting at the lawyers in Tumut, leaving Hannah in Woody's care, asking her father, BJ, to drive her to the appointment as she knew she might be too emotional to drive home.

Then, on the way back, she'd realised they had been driving behind John's car and it had been clear as he'd zoomed around the winding bends in the road that he hadn't been alone in the car, Lorelai often catching a glimpse of a woman sitting beside him. The woman who had stolen her husband.

She swallowed over her anger and pain as she carefully edged closer to the side of the road, which fell away down an embankment towards the lake.

'What about Hannah?' Lorelai asked Woody. 'If you come here, who's going to look—?'

'Hamilton's here. He's a responsible lad. I'll get him to mind your daughter. Honey and Edward are due back soon so I'm leaving a message for them.'

'OK. Hurry, Woody.'

'I'm on my way, Lorelai.' His words were strong, determined, dependable. 'Just...' He paused. 'Be careful, all right?'

'I will.' Lorelai nodded, drawing in the strength he was exuding down the phone. 'Thanks.' She disconnected the call, breathing deeply again, allowing a sense of calm to wash over her as she pushed her phone into the pocket of her jeans.

Reinforcements were on their way, her father was a trained State Emergency Services captain and together they'd be able to at least stabilise the situation. She'd attended emergencies before...but she'd never in her wildest dreams thought she'd have to treat her wayward husband and his mistress.

Unfortunately, with the winding roads along the great Snowy Mountains Highway in New South Wales, accidents like this were far too common. With all the back-up and emergency services on the way, surely that meant everything would be all right—wouldn't it?

She continued to work at steadying her heartbeat, telling herself this situation was no different from other emergencies of a similar nature. She put her bag at her feet, then wiped her perspiring hands down her jeans, but they didn't feel any drier. She closed her eyes for a moment, desperate to block out what was going to happen next, not wanting to face it but knowing she had to. When she opened her eyes again, nothing had changed. The car below still lay in a mangled heap before her. She picked up her bag and straightened her shoulders, knowing she could do this.

'Lore! Be careful. Don't touch the car at all,' her father called from above. Lorelai heeded her father's words and moved with care down the embankment towards the badly damaged car. She was still trying to come to terms with what she'd seen—John's car swerving through the barriers before tipping over the embankment.

What had John been thinking? Why had he been driving so fast? No. She didn't want an answer to that question right now. She couldn't think of all the terrible things John had done to her, of the pain he'd caused especially during the past few weeks. Right now he needed her help, her professional expertise…and so did his mistress.

Sliding on the dirt and stones beneath her shoes, Lorelai forced herself to slow down even more, watching where she was stepping otherwise she might twist her ankle and then she'd have one more obstacle to navigate. She picked her way through the shattered glass of the windscreen and when she eventually stood beside the car, which was almost on a forty-five degree angle towards the ground, the chassis of the car facing the sky, Lorelai gasped, covering her mouth with her hands as she looked at the man who was still legally her husband.

'Oh, John.' Her breathing was erratic and she shook her head, trying to keep her tears under control. She would do him no good if she lost the plot.

From what she could see, John was wedged tightly

between the seat and the steering-wheel, slumped over, still held in firmly by the seat belt, a large red gash on his head oozing blood, his legs obscured from her view by the twisted metal of the car.

Knowing that until the car was secured, it could still shift, Lorelai stepped as close as she dared, calling his name, trying to keep the fear from her tone. He may have cheated on her, he may have rejected the baby she'd only given birth to a fortnight ago, he may have caused her immeasurable pain and heartache, but he didn't deserve to die. Not like this.

She reached forward and pressed two fingers to his carotid pulse, not surprised to find it weak but thready. 'Hold on, John.' She looked past him, to the passenger seat but, surprisingly, found it empty. She frowned. She knew for a fact that his mistress had been in the car because she'd seen the other woman laughing at John as they'd driven through the streets of Tumut. John, parading around the town with his new woman in tow, in front of people they'd known for years, in front of *her*. Had he honestly cared so little for their life together?

'Lore?' Her father's deep baritone pierced her distress and she stood to see where he was. 'Over here. Quickly,' BJ called, and Lorelai reluctantly left the unconscious John, knowing at this stage there was little she could do for him.

'Who's controlling the traffic?' she called as she made her way towards him

'Ike was passing by. He's a young cadet but he knows his emergency protocols.' Her father was crouched next to something and as she drew closer, she realised it was the mistress.

'She's unconscious but she's breathing. How's John?'

'Bad. Trapped. Very bad.' She bit her tongue, trying to control her rising emotions. 'I can't…I can't see his legs, Dad.' Lorelai looked at her father, her voice wobbling on the last few words. BJ reassuringly put his hands onto her shoulders, looking into her eyes.

'There's nothing we can do for John at the moment, not until help arrives. We need to stabilise that car before I'll allow anyone near it. You understand, don't you, Lore? My first duty as an SES captain is to ensure the safety of all rescue workers.'

She nodded, the action small, her jaw clenched in an effort to control her emotions. 'I know, Dad.'

'For now, she…' he indicated the patient before them '…needs your help. Sweetheart,' BJ continued, 'I know this is difficult but you have to focus. You're a professional, Lorelai Rainbow. You're my daughter and it doesn't matter what either John or this woman—'

'Jean.' Lorelai swallowed. 'Her name is Jean.'

'Right. It doesn't matter what they've done to you, how they've hurt you, they don't deserve to die.'

Lorelai nodded, knowing her father spoke the truth. She closed her eyes and concentrated, drawing in a deep, calming breath, reminding herself that help would soon arrive, that Woody was on his way. She pushed aside her personal thoughts and pulled on her professionalism. She was a doctor. She'd taken an oath to uphold life and that was what she would do.

Opening her eyes, she nodded to her father and reached for her medical bag. 'As soon as Woody arrives, have him take a look at John,' she said, and knelt down beside the supine body of her patient. 'I have to be honest with you, Dad, even from my quick perusal and the feel of his pulse, I don't know if he'll—' She broke off, unable to say the words out loud. BJ nodded understandingly.

'You're strong, Lorelai. Stronger than you think, love.'

'You're the only man in the world who thinks so, Dad, and I love you for it.'

Twenty minutes later, all the back-up they'd requested had arrived, the SES firefighters had doused the overturned car with fire retardant and were starting to secure it with cables. BJ was organising and ordering whilst Woody was crouched down opposite her as they worked on continuing to stabilise Jean. At Lorelai's request, he'd taken a look at John but until the car was stable, BJ wasn't allowing anyone to get closer.

'I've just spoken to my sister,' he'd told her not long after he'd arrived. 'She and Edward are on their way here.'

Lorelai had sighed, pleased her two medical colleagues would be there soon. Right now, she needed all the help and support she could get. Edward was like a brother to her and Honey had become a very close friend in a very short time, so much so that it was Honey who had delivered Lorelai's baby.

As they worked together, Lorelai looked at Woody, amazed that when he'd first arrived on the scene, he hadn't demanded a report or behaved like all qualified general surgeons, in an arrogant and overbearing manner, taking charge of the case at hand. Instead, he'd assessed the situation for himself and then looked at her with admiration.

'You've done a great job of stabilising her, Lorelai.' His words were deep and calm.

She wasn't sure how he did it but just hearing his rich tone had somehow managed to sooth her frazzled nerves and settle her wayward thoughts. She was still worried about John and she was still trying to keep her professional focus as far as Jean was concerned but Woody's reassurance, his relaxed presence, as though he'd seen this sort of injury a thousand times before and knew exactly what to do, helped her to pause, draw in a cleansing breath and then slowly let it out.

'Jean's broken a lot of bones.' Woody shook his head as they finished carefully wrapping the fresh bandage around their patient's head. 'Carotid pulse is strong, which is a good sign, but with the facial lacerations she's sustained, she'll require skin grafts, plastic surgery and will be left with a multitude of scars.'

'You sound very sure of that.'

'I've seen it many times before, although on those other occasions I was usually in the jungles of Tarparnii or in Afghanistan. At least Jean has access to skilled surgeons and modern equipment.'

'You like to travel a lot, don't you?' Lorelai asked rhetorically as she performed Jean's observations again. Thankfully, with the arrival of the paramedics, they'd been able to insert an IV drip as Jean's blood pressure was still low.

'There's a big wide world out there. So much to see and do and learn,' Woody replied, although Lorelai was surprised to realise his words seemed rehearsed, as though he'd given that reply many times before. Why was that? She brushed the thought aside and concentrated on helping him to continue stabilising Jean.

'Honey said the longest you've ever stayed in one place was for two years.'

'She's right. I was thirteen years old and had fallen from a tree, landing on my back. I'd fractured my spine so spent a good deal of time in hospital. My parents couldn't give in to their wandering feet and had to stay put. It was strange, being in one place for such a long time.'

'Long time? Two years? Apart from medical school, I've lived my whole life in this very district.' She shook her head, quite bemused with his wanderlust.

'It seemed longer, especially when I was supine in traction. Not good for a teenage boy. However, I have to say being in hospital, watching the medical staff, the cleaners, the cooks, the maintenance staff, it brought to life this exciting new world. It was then I decided to become a doctor, so I guess it wasn't all bad.' He paused for a second and shook his head, clearing his thoughts of the past and focusing on the present. 'Jean's blood pressure is still low, even with the drip.'

'Internal bleeding?'

'Yes, although it can't be too bad as she's holding on.'

'She's voided, which is indicative of bladder rupture.'

'She'll need to go directly to surgery once she arrives in A and E. Will she go to Tumut or Canberra hospital?' he asked.

'She'll be taken to Tumut then airlifted to Canberra,' Lorelai supplied.

Woody nodded. 'I'll call a friend of mine who works there, let him know she's coming.' He looked down at Jean and shook his head. 'She can't have been wearing her seat belt, hence why she was thrown so far from the car,' he continued. 'And given her head injuries, it's clear she went through the windscreen. Extremely dangerous to travel in a car without wearing a seat belt.'

'I had to pull several splinters of glass from her left eye. I've flushed it as best as I could but she'll need an eye surgeon to assess it,' Lorelai stated as Woody continued to wind the bandage over Jean's face, covering the pad Lorelai had placed over the woman's left eye. The cervical collar was protecting Jean's spine and they'd splinted her other limbs, Woody's clever and experienced hands moving quickly but cautiously so as not to create further complications.

'I think we're ready to get her out of here.' Woody took the walkie-talkie BJ had given him and radioed the paramedics. 'We're ready to transfer Jean.'

'Copy that,' came the reply, and soon the paramedics had Jean secured to the stretcher. Lorelai watched as they took Jean up the embankment to the waiting ambulance. Then, for the first time since her father had asked her to focus, Lorelai allowed her mind to drift towards the man who was still legally her husband. He may have cheated on her, he may have ripped her heart out, rejecting both her and their daughter, but he was still her husband.

On legs that were trembling as she stumbled over to where John was still trapped in the mangled car, Lorelai swallowed over the sudden dryness of her throat. Firefighters were attaching cables to the car and Woody had somehow crawled into the vehicle and was monitoring John closely.

She could hear voices around her, people talking and calling instructions to each other, but they all seemed distant, far away. None of this seemed real. It was like a bad nightmare but she knew it wasn't one she could wake up from.

Lorelai swallowed. Everything around her slowed down, so much so that for a second everything seemed to stand still. She could hear no sounds, nothing except for the beating of her own heart pounding against her chest, the beat slightly faster than usual.

So much pain. So much anguish. Hot tears stung at

her eyes. John was responsible for the pain in her chest, for the tears in her eyes, for the breaking of her heart. He'd destroyed her self-esteem, her self-confidence, he'd emotionally stripped her bare and then he'd discarded her like a broken toy.

But that didn't mean he deserved to die.

The blood continued to pound in her ears and with a rush of noise the world started to turn again. She knew the chances of John surviving this accident were slim and part of her wanted to leave so she didn't have to face the inevitable—watching her husband die, knowing there wasn't a thing she could do to save him—but she didn't want to go home alone. She needed someone with her. Someone with big strong arms who would hold and protect her. She didn't have anyone like that.

It was every doctor's worst nightmare when they were unable to save the life of a loved one. She'd seen John's legs, the way the twisted metal seemed to blend with his limbs as though he was one with the car. The fact he hadn't regained consciousness, that his pulse was weak, that… Lorelai stopped her thoughts, her heart hammering against her chest. She wasn't that strong.

Woody's voice came through on the walkie-talkie, relaying John's latest set of vitals to BJ, who was at the top of the embankment, controlling the situation.

'It's not good,' she whispered into the wind. Logically, she knew it was hopeless to wish for John to survive. She wished she could change things, go back and fix her marriage, do whatever it took to keep her daughter's father alive, but she knew she couldn't. From Woody's last report, it was clear John's internal injuries were too extensive and he still hadn't regained consciousness.

The rescue teams were trying to get into position

to cut John free but with the front of the car being so crushed, it was slow going…and time was something they didn't have on their side.

All she could think about was John and the sight of him hanging upside down, his legs obscured by the mangled metal. She really didn't want to be there when the verdict finally came, being told that John simply hadn't been strong enough to pull through—yet, still, she lacked the strength to go.

Then, almost as though she was dreaming, Edward, her surrogate brother, appeared as though from thin air. Edward, her friend. He'd know what to do. Edward always knew what to do and she trusted his judgement one hundred per cent.

'Lore?' He put his medical bag down and hugged her close.

'Oh, Edward.' Tears instantly flooded over the barriers she'd worked hard to erect. 'Edward, it's John.' She sobbed into his shoulder, her professional armour finally cracking. She had no idea how long she stood there, crying on his shoulder. It could have been seconds, it might have been hours. General time was irrelevant, especially as deep down inside, she knew she was waiting for TOD—time of death—to be called.

Edward eased her back a little and it was then, as she wiped her eyes, that she realised Woody was standing beside her.

'Come on, Lorelai. Let me take you home,' Woody offered, putting his hand on her shoulders. His touch was warm, gentle, comforting.

'Good idea. Go on up with Woody,' Edward agreed softly. 'Let him take you home. Honey and I will look after John.'

Lorelai looked at him, seeing the promise and the

truth in his words. Edward had never let her down in the past and he wouldn't now. It helped to give her the strength to walk away. Edward knew John, whereas Honey had only met him once and Woody not at all. Knowing Edward was there, doing what he could to help John, lifted a heavy burden from Lorelai's shoulders and after a second of looking into his eyes, of seeing the reassurance there, she realised she could leave. Edward was family.

'OK.' She sniffed and nodded and once more wiped at the tears. She must look a sight! Glancing over at the twisted car, she took a shaky breath, said a silent goodbye, then slowly turned, allowing Woody to lead her away.

He held firmly to her hand as they walked up the embankment, ensuring she didn't slip over. They took it slowly, not wanting to rush on the loose dirt and gravel, but eventually they both made it to the top.

When they'd caught their breath, Lorelai stood to the side of the cordoned-off road and looked down at the car below. The rescue cables were in place to hold the car steady, to ensure it didn't slip any further, especially with Honey now inside the vehicle, doing her best to help John. Everyone was working hard, doing whatever they could to try and save John.

Woody's walkie-talkie crackled and hissed again in his pocket and a moment later Honey's clear tones came through.

'BJ?' Honey said, and a moment later Lorelai's father's voice crackled back.

'Honey?'

'Time of death…' Honey paused. 'Fifteen thirty-seven.'

Another moment of silence. 'Copy that,' BJ replied.

Woody looked at Lorelai but the expression on her face didn't change. 'Lorelai. I'm so sorry.' He put his arm around her shoulders. She didn't shrug him away, she didn't turn and face him, she just stopped and stared down at the car below.

Woody stood beside her, watching as all the workers stopped at Honey's news, just for a moment, out of respect. Then work started again but this time there was no need to rush. They weren't working against the clock any more.

'Goodbye, John.'

CHAPTER ONE

'MUMMY! I finished.'

Hannah's words penetrated Lorelai's thoughts but not enough to make her move. Instead, she stood before her bathroom mirror, looking unseeingly at her reflection. For the first time ever she didn't want to go to work. If she'd been working at a large hospital, she could quite easily have called in sick and no one would have been any the wiser that she wasn't really sick at all.

However, she was a partner in the small GP practice in the small sub-alpine town of Oodnaminaby and any attempt to 'chuck a sickie' would result in over half the town knocking on her door to check she was all right and the other half cooking her a meal and offering to help in any way possible. It was what she loved most about her home town, the deeply caring nature the local residents had for each other—but on days like this, when she had to face something that seemed impossible, she wished for anonymity.

'It's not fair,' she told her reflection as she snapped out of her reverie and pulled the brush through her blonde locks. She didn't have the mental strength to cope with seeing her new locum again.

Woody Moon-Pie, just over three years ago, had been a shining light, guiding her through the darkest day of her life. She'd been feeling so flat, so useless after being carelessly discarded by her husband John. And not only had Woody provided medical support at the crash site but afterwards he'd made sure she and her daughter were well cared for.

He'd shown her support and compassion. He'd made her feel as though she was still a person of worth. He'd driven her home, reunited her with her daughter and then made sure she was safe throughout the evening. All she'd needed had been an anchor, someone to cling to during those first few horrific hours when her life had dramatically changed.

Woody had been attentive and kind, helping to restore her faith in the opposite sex, to let her see there were good men out there, men who weren't deceptive and negative. When she'd been at the darkest point in her life, Woody had shared his light with her and the memory of that night had made an enormous difference to her mental and emotional recovery.

It was why she'd often found herself thinking about him, wondering where he was, what he was doing and sometimes even dreaming about him.

The Woody of her dreams was every inch the hero, riding into town on his white horse, scooping her up into his arms and asking her where she had been all his life. It was a fantasy—nothing more—which was why she was incredibly embarrassed at the thought of facing the *real* Woody in just under half an hour.

The fact that Woody was starting work at the Oodnaminaby Family Medical Practice today was most definitely the reason why she'd been thinking about him a lot lately. While she kept telling herself that he meant nothing to her, that he was simply the brother of her best friend, who had played the part of knight in shining armour for one evening, she couldn't help the nervous apprehension she was feeling, knowing she'd be seeing him soon.

She was sure that during the past three years Woody hadn't even given her a second thought. Even the reason Woody was in Oodnaminaby wasn't anything to do with her. His sister, Honey, was five months pregnant and wanted to take a few months off work so she and her husband, Edward, could do some travelling before the birth of their baby. Woody had volunteered to come help out at the clinic for as long as was necessary and Lorelai was the one left to deal with the handsome surgeon.

'Mummy?' Hannah's voice rang out, tinged with a hint of impatience. When you were three and one quarter, you tended not to have a lot of patience.

'Coming,' Lorelai called back, and went to help her daughter off the toilet. 'I don't think it's fair that I have to put up with the stress of toilet training as well as dealing with Woody's enigmatic presence,' she grumbled to herself as she sorted Hannah out. Hannah's reply was to promptly put her arms around her mother's neck and press a big sloppy kiss to her cheek.

'I love you oodles and squoodles, Mummy,' Hannah remarked, before going to wash her hands. Lorelai stood for a moment, shaking her head in wonderment, a bright smile on her face.

'You always know the perfect thing to say to help Mummy,' she told her daughter. It didn't matter what the day would bring, she had Hannah, and therefore, everything else was immaterial.

* * *

'Is that coffee I smell?' Woody walked into his sister's kitchen, snagging a piece of toast that had just popped up.

'Hey. That was mine,' Honeysuckle Goldmark protested, and rubbed her pregnant belly. 'Think of your unborn niece or nephew. How could you? Mean uncle.'

Woody chuckled as he buttered the toast, accepting the cup of coffee his sister handed him. 'I promise to never steal food from your child—once he or she is born,' Woody promised. 'However, *your* food, big sister, is fair game.'

Honey swatted at him with a tea-towel but he quickly shifted out the way. 'Rotter,' she said.

'Are you teasing my pregnant wife?' Edward asked as he came in through the back door in his stockinged feet, his shoes left just outside the door. He undid his coat and took it off, hanging it over the back of a chair.

'No. I'm teasing my pregnant sister,' Woody returned, watching as his brother-in-law instantly crossed to Honey's side and kissed her on the lips before bending down and kissing her swollen abdomen. He couldn't be happier for his sister and to see her glowing with joy, it gave him hope. Maybe one day… Woody shook his head, stopping his thoughts from travelling in that particular direction. 'So, how's the weather this morning? Any snowfall overnight?'

'Only a light sprinkling,' Edward replied, wrapping his arms about his wife. 'It's more slushy out there now.'

'You two drive carefully,' Woody said, his tone holding a slight warning.

'And you be nice to Lorelai,' Honey retorted.

'What? Me? I'm always nice to everyone I meet, especially Lorelai. We really connected last time I was in town.' Perhaps a little too well, but he wasn't about to tell his sister that. Confessing something like that to Honey would only make her ask a lot of questions he was nowhere near ready to answer.

'The last time you were in town was possibly the worst time of her life.'

'And I was thoughtful and sensitive and supportive,' he pointed out.

'But you left without saying goodbye.' Edward's tone held no hint of teasing, his words soft and filled with meaning. Woody knew that although they weren't blood relations, Edward and his brothers looked upon Lorelai as the sister they'd never had. As such, they were all highly protective of her. 'She was upset about that.'

Woody tried to shrug his shoulders in a nonchalant way but didn't quite pull it off. Lorelai had been upset he hadn't said goodbye? But why? He knew he didn't mean anything to her and he'd also thought that after the horror she'd been through in facing her husband's death, the last person she'd want to have hanging around was the one who'd seen her at her worst—namely him.

'I was called back to Tarparnii so I thought it best to leave straight away.' He took another bite of his toast.

'Hmm.' Honey shook her head, watching him closely. 'So you've told me before but I can't help thinking there's more to it than that.' She sipped her herbal tea, glancing at the clock. 'Oh, help. Is that the time?' She put her cup down. 'We'd best get going,' she told Edward. 'Right after I go to the loo. The baby's jumping on my bladder.'

'Again?' Edward said with a smile on his face, as his wife quickly kissed her brother goodbye and then rushed from the room.

'I'd best be heading off, too. Don't want to be late for my first day on the job.' He finished his toast and coffee before stacking his dishes in the dishwasher. 'Have to keep in Lorelai's good books.'

'Yes, you do.' There was a protective tone in Edward's voice. 'Lore finally has her life back on track. The past three years haven't been easy but she's strong.'

'She always has been. Any doctor who can push aside personal feelings to provide emergency medical care to the woman who stole her husband is a permanent heroine in my books.' With a final nod towards his brother-in-law, Woody headed to the closet to collect his coat, scarf and gloves. 'Travel safe and stay in touch.'

'Will do,' Edward said with a wave.

As Woody stepped outside, the briskness of the morning surrounded him as he breathed in the cool air. After being acclimatised to the Tarparniian humidity, winter was something of a novelty. He blew steam with his mouth. 'Excellent.'

Just over three years ago when he'd arrived in Oodnaminaby for a one-week holiday with his sister—and to check out the man who had stolen his sister's heart—Woody had become quite familiar with the small sub-alpine town.

Back then it had been summer and he'd walked most of these streets before, having been invited out to dinner almost every night of his visit. When Honey and Edward had gone out of town for a few days, he'd filled in at the clinic and now he walked the same route towards the building situated in the small block of shops that was the hub of the town.

It was a lovely town and a place where he'd instantly felt at home. That had been odd for him given for the past few years he hadn't even called Australia home. His work had taken him to the pacific island nation of

Tarparnii where he'd ended up staying far longer than he'd initially planned.

But that was long ago—another lifetime ago—and even though it had been almost four years since tragedy had struck his life, he was still finding it difficult to move forward. Being back in Oodnaminaby, filling in for Edward and Honey once more, was the diversion he'd been looking for. The only concern that had made him hesitate marginally when Honey had first asked him to locum for them had been Lorelai.

The last time he'd been in town there had been a strange sort of connection between them. He couldn't explain it and he certainly didn't understand it but often, during the past three years, when his world had, at times, seemed impossible to navigate, he'd thought of Lorelai. Her strength, her resolve, the way she'd slightly lift her chin, defiance in her baby-blue eyes. She had real gumption, something he'd always admired about her.

On a whim, he veered off course and headed down the street where Lorelai lived, secretly hoping he'd bump into her. He had no idea what time she left for the clinic, no idea where Hannah stayed whilst her mother was at work, no idea whether there was someone new in her life.

Over the years, whenever his sister had mentioned anything to do with Lorelai and Hannah, Woody had been attentive to every detail. However, he couldn't recall Honey mentioning a man in Lorelai's life. Why that should lighten his heart, he had no idea. He'd tried a deep, lasting relationship once before and it had ended in tragedy. He wasn't looking to go down that track again any time soon.

Still, there was no denying he felt something for

Lorelai and he wasn't exactly sure why. However, he was in no position to follow through on any attraction he might feel for her. He had responsibilities elsewhere, people depending on him for their very survival, and it wasn't fair for him to ask any woman to endure that.

'Tum on, Mummy.'

Woody looked towards the sound of the cute little voice, watching as a little girl of about three came to the edge of the footpath and even though there were no cars out on this brisk morning, she stopped at the kerb and waited.

It was Hannah. Although he hadn't seen the child since she was a wee babe, the resemblance to her beautiful mother was unmistakeable, even though she was bundled up in her winter woollies. What a good girl she was, waiting for her mother. He could see she was wearing a pink coat, a purple and red scarf with matching gloves and beanie with little blonde curls peeking out between the collar of the coat and the edge of the beanie. He slowed his pace, watching intently as he drew closer to Lorelai's house.

'We be late for Tonnie's,' the child persisted, and for a moment Woody thought she might stamp her little foot with impatience. A smile lit his eyes at the defiance. Of course Lorelai's daughter would have as much strength, confidence and tenacity as her mother.

'I'm coming.'

At the sound of Lorelai's voice, Woody was surprised at the thrill of anticipation coursing through him. A moment later he heard a front door close. He held his breath, waiting, waiting for that first glimpse. A fraction of a second passed before he caught sight of the one woman who had often given him pause. He slowly exhaled as he watched her walk towards her daughter, his steps slowing down even further. She had her arms full, her coat all bunched up around her neck as though she hadn't yet found a second to settle the collar. A large handbag hung off one arm, the other held a purple and pink backpack, a red scarf and a set of keys.

Her blonde hair was loose, tumbling around her face but shining golden in the winter sun. It was shorter now than it had been the last time he'd seen her, the cool breeze teasing the ends as she helped Hannah to put on her backpack. Then she stood and started adjusting her coat collar, righting herself before looping the scarf around her neck and hefting her bag onto her shoulder.

It was only then she turned and saw him.

Woody's smile was instant and he was amazed that after all this time it didn't seem as though Lorelai had aged a single second. She still looked incredibly beautiful, even more so if that was at all possible. For one brief second his throat became thick with longing, his body filled with excitement at the vision of loveliness before him. He quickly squashed it and cleared his throat.

'Top of the mornin' to ya.' Woody brought his hand to his forehead in a loose salute, which ended in a wave. His smile was bright and welcoming, his eyes fixed on hers.

'Woody!' She couldn't help the blush that tinged her cheeks at seeing him again. The last time she'd seen him she'd been a mess, physically and emotionally. His bright smile also had the added effect of elevating her heart rate. She ignored it. Woody was here to help out, to work. He was a colleague. Nothing more. 'Hi.'

'Hi, yourself.' He grinned brightly, his teeth almost as white as the snow that had fallen last night. 'On your way to the clinic?'

'Er…yes, but…um, I have to drop Hannah at a friend's place first.'

'Hannah?' Woody opened his eyes wide as he came to stand beside them on the footpath. 'Good heavens.' He immediately crouched down so he was closer to Hannah's height. 'This can't possibly be baby Hannah. She's grown up so fast and she's three times as beautiful now as she was back then.'

'I *am* Hannah.' The little girl nodded enthusiastically and held up three fingers. 'I'm free and a quarter.'

'Wow. Three *and* a quarter. What a big girl you are.'

Hannah nodded again and Lorelai could see her daughter was quickly smitten with the man before her.

'Well, Hannah, my name is Woody.' He held out his gloved hand to her and with all the flourish of royalty Hannah placed her hand in his. Woody dutifully raised her gloved hand to his lips and kissed it. Hannah giggled at the gesture.

'You funny, Woody.'

'Thank you.' He glanced up at Lorelai. 'I do try to please my audience.' He was rewarded with one of Lorelai's dazzling, mind-blowing smiles for his efforts.

'I saw a photo of you,' Hannah told him, eager to keep his attention on her.

'Really? Where?'

'Aunty Honey showed me.'

'Ah. Of course she did.'

'You her little bruvver.' Hannah studied him for a moment. 'But how come you so big, then? You bigger than Aunty Honey.'

Woody chuckled. 'That's right. I am her little big brother. Sometimes boys grow bigger than girls but Aunty Honey is much, much, *much* older than me.'

'By three years,' Lorelai announced, and shook her

head. 'If Honey were here, she'd no doubt punch you in the arm.'

Woody stood and angled his shoulder towards her, pleased that his first meeting with Lorelai seemed to be progressing quite smoothly. 'You'd better do the honours, for Honey's sake if nothing else.'

Lorelai smiled and shook her head. 'Still the joker.' Even as she said the words she knew that was only one part of his personality she'd been enamoured with last time they'd met. Through the circumstances of her husband's death Lorelai had been privileged to witness a deeper, more personal side to Woody. However, it would do her well to forget about it and treat Woody as she treated all her surrogate brothers. Pretending he was just another member of the Goldmark clan should do well in controlling any frisson of awareness she might experience in his presence.

'We not allowed to hit people,' Hannah pointed out, and Woody instantly sobered and nodded.

'Quite right, too. I can see you're just as smart as your mother and every bit as lovely.' He glanced at Lorelai as he spoke, his gaze lingering on her for only a second but it was enough to reignite the slow burn Lorelai had been trying to douse all morning. She thought her knees might actually give way if he kept looking at her any longer and tried frantically to get her brain in gear.

'Uh…we need to keep going or we'll be late,' she quickly interjected, needing to move, to shift, to do anything in order to put a bit of distance between herself and Woody.

'Late? This is Oodnaminaby, Lorelai. The place takes only fifteen minutes to walk around—and that's the circumference of the town! I know, I timed it last time

I was here.' He smiled as he straightened up. 'I think you'll be fine.'

'We going to Tonnie's,' Hannah told him with a nod, before shaking her head. 'We tarn't be late.'

'Oh! Well, in that case, you're going to need a magic carpet to ride on.' Hannah's big blue eyes widened at Woody's words, as did her mother's.

'A what?' Lorelai asked, stunned and amazed at the way Hannah felt completely comfortable with Woody. Even though Woody had indeed known Hannah since she was a baby and even though he was Honey's brother, which brought with it a certain level of trust, Hannah had always been very cautious around strangers.

Woody laughed, then quickly bent down and scooped Hannah, backpack and all, off her feet and onto his shoulders. The little girl squealed with delight and clapped her hands before spreading her arms out wide. 'A magic carpet. Which way shall we fly today?' he asked, holding firmly to Hannah's legs before heading off down the street, leaving Lorelai to stare in stunned disbelief.

She watched as her daughter pretended to fly the 'magic carpet', the little girl no stranger to shoulder rides as Uncle Edward and grandpa BJ often gave her rides, teaching her how to balance properly without the need to clutch their heads.

As she followed them down the street, Lorelai wondered if Woody had chosen to walk down her street on purpose. There was a more direct route from Honey's and Edward's home to the clinic yet for some reason he'd walked down *her* street. Deep down she wondered whether he'd come this way in the hope that he might bump into her.

Ridiculous. She shook her head, pushing away the

fanciful thought. Men like Woody Moon-Pie didn't fawn over women like her. He was a man of the world, always travelling, always heading off on a new adventure, while she was happy here, at her home, with her daughter.

Apart from when Woody had been here last, he hadn't been back to Oodnaminaby. He had kept in close contact with his sister, though, and Honey would often share the news with Lorelai.

'Woody's over in Afghanistan,' or, 'Woody's just returned from Japan,' or, 'Woody sent a postcard from Mozambique,' Honey would often announce. Sometimes there would be great stories to tell, especially of his escapades in Tarparnii—a place where he seemed to spend at least six months of the year—and Honey's eyes would be so alive with happiness that Lorelai found herself drawn in, wanting to hear about Woody's latest news. 'He called last night and told me about the most amazing thing that happened to him.' Then Honey would relate stories so wild and crazy and scary and downright funny that Lorelai was either gasping in shock or clutching her sides with laughter.

Woody was undoubtedly the most daring, exciting and incredibly sexy man Lorelai had ever met...and he'd seen her at her worst. Whenever she reflected on that night, she remembered it had been difficult for her to cry, difficult to think of what her future might hold, difficult to believe what was really happening. She'd felt incredibly numb, her mouth dry, her limbs heavy.

He'd helped her, there was no doubt about that. He'd been supportive, that wasn't in question either. He'd restored her faith in the opposite sex merely by being thoughtful and considerate but that was who he was.

She was nothing special to him—just another person he'd helped through a terrible time.

Even when Honey had related stories about Woody's escapades, such as when he'd been part of the medical team to assist in the aftermath of a tsunami, and he'd carried two young children on his back whilst helping their mother to navigate the waist-deep waters...or when Honey had told her about Woody spending the night in a cave, keeping a badly injured teenage boy company while the rescue crews had figured out the safest way to extract their patient.

He was clearly good at all the knight-in-shining-armour stuff and was able to polish his breastplate quite often, going to different countries and helping out where needed. It meant she was nothing special to him, nothing more than one of his sister's closest friends, and anything else she might have read into that night, so long ago, was irrelevant to him working here now.

That point had been made abundantly clear to her when she'd woken, the morning after John's death, to find Woody had left. She'd heard Honey's voice coming from the kitchen so knew she wasn't alone in the house but when she'd enquired after Woody, Honey had told her that he'd had to leave.

It had taken Lorelai a while to realise he hadn't just left her house to go and shower and refresh himself, as she'd initially thought, but instead he'd left Oodnaminaby. That's when shame and embarrassment had zipped through her. Up until then, she'd thought they'd found some sort of connection, that in caring for her and Hannah, Woody had felt something deeper. With a thud she'd realised he'd just been doing his job and that she'd fallen victim to a reverse Florence Nightingale effect.

Woody had gone…returned to his life and hadn't been back in Oodnaminaby since… Until now.

Lorelai shook her head. She'd been foolish back then but she wouldn't be foolish now, not when she had Hannah to think about. Woody continued down the street, his steps sure and steadfast as he gave Hannah her magic carpet ride to Connie's house. Lorelai could hear Hannah chattering away, her sweet voice carrying easily through the crisp July morning.

It was one thing for Lorelai to be all silly, remembering the effects of Woody's natural charm, but it was quite another for him to use his charm on Hannah.

Allowing her daughter to form an attachment to the man who had no home, who was a drifter, who she doubted would ever want to settle down in one place for the rest of his life, would be disastrous.

Lorelai had made big mistakes in the romance department once before. Her marriage to John, she'd realised years later, had been nothing but a farce. He'd wanted a woman who was self-sufficient, who earned enough money for him to leech off and who lived close to his one true love—the snowfields. Skiing had been John's favourite thing to do and during winter he'd refused to work at his job as a demolition expert, preferring to live off the joint bank account Lorelai had set up when they'd married. She'd been fortunate that he hadn't had access to all her accounts, otherwise he would have left her with nothing.

During the past three years since his death, she'd come to realise what she'd been looking for had been stability, someone who would always be there for her and Hannah to rely on. Quite simply, with the way Woody had left three years ago and the way he seemed to travel the world, Lorelai knew he was the last person she should ever consider in a romantic light.

'He's just another brother type. That's all. Nothing special about him whatsoever.'

Yet even as she followed Woody and Hannah down the street, she knew she was fooling no one.

CHAPTER TWO

'OH, he's just as lovely as I remember,' Ginny told Lorelai when the two of them met up in the kitchenette, the receptionist's cheeks tinged with pink as she spoke. 'And I think he's even more handsome than when he was here last time. Don't you think?'

'Uh…yes.' The last thing Lorelai wanted to do was to arouse any suspicions that she'd indulged in a bit of hero-worship where Woody was concerned, so thought it best simply to agree with Ginny, finish making her tea and head back to her consulting room. Just as she stepped into the corridor, she saw Woody come out from his room with Mrs Peterson in tow. He chatted patiently with the blushing seventy-three-year-old as she slowly manoeuvred her walking frame towards the waiting-room area.

'You're so right, young man. I *do* need to be looking after myself more. I'll look forward to your home visits and I promise to faithfully do my leg exercises. You'll see a big improvement when you come in three days' time.' Mrs Peterson nodded. 'Just you wait and see.'

Woody smiled at her. 'I'm looking forward to it as well.' He stopped by the empty reception desk as though only then realising Ginny wasn't there. 'Oh. Just a moment, Mrs Peterson. I'll see if I can loca—' He stopped as Ginny almost came sprinting down the corridor.

'I'm here. I'm here,' she called, having pushed past Lorelai so quickly Lorelai thought *Ginny* might break her hip. The receptionist had been a motherly figure to Lorelai for most of her life and it was odd to see her so flustered around Woody and his hypnotic good looks.

Not only did his handsome face set the female population of Ood a-twitter but his charming manner and easy humour had the ability to cause cheeks to flush and hearts to thump a bit faster. He would hold doors for his patients, helping them to their seats. He would make direct eye contact with them, listening intently to all they had to say. He would answer all questions quite patiently and provide answers that were couched in layman's terms so that people clearly understood what was happening.

Lorelai could quite see why every female in the town was flustered in his presence. Even *she*'d had trouble keeping herself under control during the past week since he'd arrived in town. Hannah had taken an instant shine to him, something that had caused Lorelai more than a moment of concern. Woody was only scheduled to be in town until Honey and Edward returned—whenever that might be. After their return, she had no doubt he'd pull his disappearing act again, heading off to goodness only knew where without a word of farewell to anyone.

That's what he'd done three years ago and even now Lorelai was surprised at how hurt she'd felt. Back then, with her state of mind being in total disarray, she'd thought she'd done something wrong to make Woody leave the way he had.

Now, having had years to think about it, she knew his leaving had had nothing to do with her. She'd also realised what she'd felt for him that night had been nothing but gratitude. He'd stayed with her and Hannah, making sure they were safe during her darkest hours. For that she truly was grateful but that didn't mean she was going to let her daughter become so attached to Woody during this visit that she'd be heart-broken when he left.

'Almost ready to go?' Woody leaned against the wall in the corridor, facing Lorelai. 'Hello?' He waved a hand in front of her face. 'Lore? Are you in there?'

Lorelai moved her head back, only then realising she was still standing in the doorway of the kitchenette and he wasn't in the reception area any more but instead was right before her. 'Sorry,' she murmured, looking down at the tea in her mug, slightly embarrassed at being caught daydreaming. She searched her thoughts, trying to figure out what he'd asked her. 'Ah…house calls. That's right. I need to show you the ropes. Yes, I'll be ready in about ten minutes.' She sipped at her tea and then headed towards her consulting room. 'Just need to finalise things from today's clinic, grab the house-call files from Ginny and pack the medical bag.'

'I can do the last two. You get all caught up on your consulting notes and then we'll head off. I presume we're taking your car because it already knows the way?'

'Knows the way?'

'To where we're going.' Woody shook his head. 'Catch up, Lorelai.' Then, with a wink, he headed back out to Reception, no doubt to fluster Ginny further.

With a look he could set Lorelai's heart racing. With a wink he could make her knees turn to mush. With the sound of his deep laughter reverberating in her ears, he could make her entire body tingle with delight—*and* he was considerate. Lorelai wasn't sure just how she was supposed to keep her thoughts under control when her body was clearly reacting to him.

'Just another brother. He's just another brother,' she repeated as she headed into her clinic room. It was OK to think your brother was handsome, wasn't it? She certainly thought of the Goldmark boys as handsome but not her type. She could think of Woody in exactly the same, familial way.

Yet as she sat down to write up her notes, she found her thoughts returning to the way Woody smiled, the way he winked and the way he set her insides alight in a way that made her feel *anything* but sisterly towards him.

Half an hour later, after Lorelai had shown Woody the best way to attach the snow chains to the tyres of her car, they made their way towards Pleasing Valley, which was a small village not too far away from the snowfields but situated below the snowline. 'I'm sure I went to Pleasing Valley three years ago and it didn't take this long,' Woody commented after they'd been in the car for well over an hour.

'It's winter now. Everything takes twice as long as it does in summer. We can't get to Pleasing Valley through the hills. We have to go through Jindabyne and then head out.'

'I thought Honey said the Oodnaminaby practice usually shared house-call rotas with the doctors in Jindabyne, especially during the winter months?'

'We do. We combine with Jindabyne and Corryong practices during winter as the influx in tourists and day-travellers to and from the snowfields tends to make things a little crazier than usual. With the extra patients, it can make it not only difficult to finish clinics on time but also to do house calls, and with an ever-increasing elderly population in these districts, we doctors need to be vigilant in our care for them. So we share the house-call roster and this week it's our turn.'

'What about if one of your patients contacts you and it's not your week?'

'Fair question. It's all circumstantial. You need to take into consideration who the patient is and whether or not it's better for them to see you rather than a different doctor. The weather is a big factor—is it snowing, raining, slushing? What's the medical complaint? Can it wait or is it urgent? And it also depends on what our own workload is like. Take today, for example. Afternoon clinic all finished by four o'clock. If there are any emergencies while we're doing these house calls, Ginny will send the patients to Tumut hospital, which, as you know, is about half an hour from Ood.'

'And Tumut's the closest hospital?'

'To us. There's a bigger hospital in Cooma and one in Corryong too but for the most part our patients either go to Tumut or, in very bad cases, are airlifted to Canberra. Tumut hospital mainly handles obstetrics, A and E and a few elective lists.' She was glad her vehicle was four-wheel-drive and switched on the windscreen wipers as snow began to fall.

'So there are no permanent surgical consultants there? Residents?'

'Not on a regular daily basis, no.' Lorelai glanced over at him. 'Why so many questions?'

Woody shrugged. 'Just trying to get a feel for the area. Goodness knows how long Honey and Edward will be away.' There was a hint of teasing humour in his words. 'You might be stuck with me far longer than you originally thought.' He chuckled, the rich sound washing over her. His tone was so deep and firm it almost vibrated through her, making her catch her breath.

Lorelai frowned, instantly annoyed with herself for being so receptive to him. It wasn't what she wanted. While she hoped Honey and Edward had a wonderful time on their travels, and while she knew they rightfully deserved the break given both of them worked hard in the Oodnaminaby Family Medical Practice, she couldn't help but wish them to return sooner rather than later. She focused her thoughts on driving, knowing it was safer than dwelling on the erratic way Woody seemed to affect her. He was looking out the window, almost mesmerised by the snow.

'This is glorious!' Woody remarked, and before she knew what he was doing, he'd wound down the window, put his head out and opened his mouth.

'What are you doing?' Lorelai asked, making sure she kept a clear watch on the road but glancing across at him from time to time. 'You look like a dog with your tongue hanging out like that.' To her chagrin, she couldn't help but laugh as he eventually pulled his head in and wound up the window. 'You're completely insane, Woody.'

'This is my first real time in the snow. This past week has been brilliant. I've been outside, making snow angels on the ground. I've had a snow-fight with some of the high-school kids in the town and even ran around my sister's back yard stark naked at midnight simply because I'd never before played in the snow in my birthday suit.'

'Really?' Lorelai's eyes widened as images of Woody's tall, naked body running around in the snow in his sister's back yard came instantly to mind. The image was enough to distract her, but only for a split second. She shook her head, needing to clear her thoughts and concentrate on driving. 'You are certifiably crazy, Dr Moon-Pie.'

'Only compared to some,' he rationalised. 'Well, I've been living in hot or humid climates for most my life.'

'That's right. I remember Honey telling me the two of you were mainly raised in far north Queensland and the Northern Territory. Added to that, haven't you spent a lot of time in the jungles of Tarparnii?'

Woody paused for a moment, giving her a sideways glance. 'Honey told you about Tarparnii?' He seemed a little surprised.

'Sure. She would often tell me about your travels. She'd sit and show Hannah pictures of you in different places, or share the postcards you'd send. Everyone in the town knows about your travels.'

'My *travels*. Ah…right. Good.' He nodded and seemed to relax. 'Yes, I'm sure she's told everyone about my travels.'

'Why? What did you think she'd said?'

'Uh…nothing.' Woody shrugged but Lorelai sensed there was more to it.

'Honey's very proud of you, Woody, and after everyone in town met you, they'd always ask after you. Small towns are caring places.'

'That's what I like about them. They're like little communities. Everyone taking care of everyone else.'

'Is that what it's like in Tarparnii?'

'It is, actually.' His natural smile was back again and Lorelai wondered whether she'd imagined his moment of concern.

'How long *were* you in Tarparnii?' Her tone was filled with curiosity.

'Which time?' he asked, looking out the window. The snow had stopped falling but Lorelai still had the windscreen wipers on. Woody reached out his hand and flicked them off for her.

'How many times have you been?'

'Too many to count. The first time was almost ten years ago. I was a medical student, lending a helping hand and ready to save the world.' Woody shook his head. 'I was so green. My first day in a country in the grip of war and I had bullets whizzing past my head.'

'What? Really?'

'I kid you not. If it hadn't been for K'nai, my Tarparnese contact, I would have been dead. No more Woody-Gum Moon-Pie.' He was silent for a moment and Lorelai realised he was lost in thought. It was obvious, given the way he was highly reflective at the mention of Tarparnii, he'd undergone quite a few life-changing experiences there.

'I thought things had settled down there recently, that the fighting wasn't so bad.'

Woody nodded. 'There has been progress in the political arena and you're right, the fighting isn't so bad. That first trip was the exception, not the rule. I've never been shot at since.'

'Good to know.' Lorelai eased the car into a lower gear and started to drive down a steep descent, drawing closer to Pleasing Valley. 'I take it you have many friends there.'

'Yes. Many good and dear friends, both local and from around the world who are over there to help out. The plight of the country is becoming more well known and foreign aid is increasing, so that's good.'

'I remember seeing a documentary on Tarparnii a few years ago. It looks like a beautiful place.'

'It is. The most picturesque countryside. You'd love it, Dr Rainbow.' He smiled as they drove along. 'Do you realise,' he said a few minutes later, 'that your name is incredibly pretty? Lorelai Rainbow.'

Lorelai was a little stunned by his forthright words. 'Er...thanks.' She knew she probably shouldn't be surprised as he *was* Honey's brother and Honey was always open and honest. It stood to reason Woody would be the same.

'What's your middle name?'

'Emily. The same as Hannah's. We're both named after my mother.'

'Lorelai Emily Rainbow. Very pretty.' He angled his head to the side and watched her for a moment. Lorelai began to shift in her seat, starting to get a little uncomfortable with his gently scrutiny. 'Do you mind if I ask, why didn't you change your name when you married John?'

Lorelai blinked, taking a moment to mentally change gears. She'd been so interested in asking him questions, of hearing the love for Tarparnii in his voice, that for a second he'd thrown her when he'd mentioned John. 'Well...uh...professionally, my degree was in the name of Rainbow. I had intended to change my name, I'd even filled out the forms, but I'd never found the time to lodge them. Then I discovered I was pregnant and it was all I could do to keep up with work and morning sickness. And now, of course, it seems better that I didn't change my name.'

Woody cast her a worried glance. Great, the last thing she needed was his sympathy or concern. She really was glad she hadn't changed her name. In the end it had made things simpler.

Clearing her throat, she watched the road, keeping

her tone light once more. 'Do you want to guess whether your sister is carrying a boy or a girl?'

Woody's smile instantly returned to his handsome face and Lorelai was both pleased and annoyed to feel that now familiar little fluttering of excitement in the pit of her stomach. She quickly dismissed the sensation as they started to discuss the various different old wives' tales in figuring out whether it was a boy or girl.

'Are you excited to be an uncle?' Lorelai slowed the car as she turned off the main road. They were almost at Pleasing Valley and although she knew these roads very well, it was still wise to take her time.

'I am. I intend to spoil the kid rotten, giving it lots of sweeties and loud noisy toys and then disappearing into the sunset to let my sister go quietly insane from the sugar-high, cymbal-banging toddler.'

Lorelai smiled. 'Well, please don't practise on my daughter.' She drove into the driveway of the first house and pulled on the handbrake. 'Hannah is noisy enough and spoilt by her uncles, aunts and grandfather as it is. She doesn't need any more.'

'You ruin all my fun,' he joked as she switched off the engine. Both of them climbing from the vehicle. Woody reached for the medical bag while Lorelai went to the rear of her car and took out a snow shovel. 'What are you doing?' he asked, standing there, watching her. Lorelai pointed to the mound of snow blocking the path to the house they were visiting.

'How do you expect to reach Mrs Maddison's front door? I'm not a fan of slipping on frozen snow and ice. Besides, with her recent hip replacement, Mrs Maddison can hardly do it.'

'So you not only provide elite medical care, you also work part time as a snow plough?'

'Only on patient driveways. I gave up doing main roads once I'd finished medical school,' she joked as Woody handed her the medical bag and took the snow shovel from her.

'Allow me.'

'It's OK, Woody. I'm quite capable of—'

'Shh. I'm being gallant,' he pointed out, and with that turned and shovelled the snow out the way. By the time he reached the door a few minutes later, he was nicely warm. 'Milady,' he said with a sweeping bow. 'Your patient awaits.'

Lorelai couldn't help but smile, enjoying the easy-going side of his personality. 'Why thank you, kind sir. You are most generous to have saved me from such a manual, bothersome task.'

Woody's eyes were brightened by the exercise, his cheeks tinged with pink, his lips curved into a smile revealing straight, white teeth. 'Anything for you, milady.' With that, he bowed again as Lorelai walked towards him, giggling at his silliness. She rang the doorbell and while they waited for Mrs Maddison, they both grinned goofily at each other.

Slowly their smiles started to slip as they simply stood and stared. From the first moment she'd met Woody at a family dinner two weeks after Hannah had been born, she'd felt a tiny undercurrent of awareness towards him. Of course, back then she'd been in the throes of her own personal drama, with her husband not only refusing to have anything to do with Hannah but also wanting her to pay him far more than he deserved in their divorce. Still, when Woody had walked into her life and smiled at her for the first time, Lorelai had felt a stirring of attraction. That stirring was well and truly flowing between them right now, so many years later.

What it all might mean she had absolutely no clue and wasn't even sure she wanted to find out.

At the rattling of the doorhandle, both Lorelai and Woody turned their attention to their patient on the other side. Woody was more than happy for the interruption as the way Lorelai had been looking at him made him feel highly uncomfortable. It wasn't the first time he'd experienced such a sensation when looking at his new colleague. It had happened three years ago when he'd first arrived in Oodnaminaby and been introduced to her.

She'd cradled Hannah in one arm, then held out her free hand to him as Honey had introduced them. The instant they'd touched, it was as though a spark of excitement had zipped through him and all from a simple handshake. When he'd looked down into Lorelai's face, he'd seen his own bewilderment mirrored in her reflection.

'Hello, Lorelai,' Mrs Maddison said as she opened the door, leaning on her walking frame for support. 'Oh, and, look, you've shovelled my walk. You shouldn't have worried, dear.'

'It was no trouble, Mrs Maddison,' Lorelai remarked as she headed into the lovely warm home. 'I brought a big, strapping young man along with me today. He made short work of the task.'

Mrs Maddison welcomed them into her home, Woody waiting patiently for Mrs Maddison to head back to her comfortable chair in the lounge room and watching her gait as she walked.

'How long ago did you have your hip replacement?' he asked.

'Almost eight weeks now,' she replied, and he could

hear the pride in her voice. 'Aren't I walking well? Lorelai says I'm doing fabulous.'

'And you are,' Lorelai remarked as she disappeared into the kitchen. 'I'll pop the kettle on. Woody can entertain you.'

'Ooh, I'd like that,' Mrs Maddison said with a little giggle. Lorelai listened to the conversation going on in the other room as she prepared a tea-tray, finding some biscuits in the cupboard. She'd needed a bit of breathing space from Woody, especially after the look they'd just shared. She closed her eyes for a moment, unable to believe after all these years the attraction was still there, zinging between them, enticing them both to explore and to taste.

When they'd met three years ago, she'd thought it had only been her who had felt that instant tug of awareness. Then, as her life had been in turmoil, she'd locked the sensation up and put it into a secret cupboard in her mind, taking the memory out and dusting it off whenever she was struck with a sense of loneliness. Meeting Woody, experiencing that initial awareness, had boosted her ego but until just now she hadn't really known whether he truly felt it too.

Last week she'd thought her reaction to him had just been a mixture of excited nerves and past embarrassment. She'd watched him charm every woman he'd come into contact with, young and old, throughout the week. Even the men had taken to him, and she'd known that keeping her distance was the right thing to do. Professional. They would be colleagues and acquaintances and nothing more.

Until he'd looked into her eyes. Sharing that moment with him had been as though they'd both acknowledged the attraction openly. The realisation both scared and excited her. She knew Woody could be wonderful and charming and a little bit flirty but she also knew taking that flirtation seriously would only end in pain…and she'd been through enough pain. Somehow she'd have to put up barriers, to ward off the effects of his bright smiles and hypnotic eyes.

The kettle boiled, bringing her out of her reverie, and with a straight back and a firm resolve she carried the tea-tray through to the lounge room. The three of them sat around, politely drinking tea and nibbling on biscuits, before Lorelai whisked Mrs Maddison away to her room for a check-up.

Woody tidied up the dishes whilst waiting for the two women, washing the cups and saucers, drying the plates and finding out where everything went. He was looking at a photograph of Mrs Maddison when she'd been much younger, a Tarparniian man standing beside her, his arm about her small, slim shoulders, when the women walked back into the room.

'Ahh, that's my Ni'juk.' Mrs Maddison shifted her walker to come and stand beside him. She lifted a loving hand towards the frame, her frail fingers reaching out as though she desperately wanted time to rewind.

'He's Tarparniian,' Woody stated with a hint of incredulity as Lorelai sat down at the kitchen bench to write up her examination notes.

'Why, yes. Have you been to Tarparnii?' Mrs Maddison was intrigued.

'Many times. I have…' Woody stopped, a sad smile on his lips '…wonderful memories of the place.'

Lorelai stopped, pen poised as she heard a haunting wistfulness in Woody's tone. She turned to watch him.

'Ah, that sounds as though you fell in love.'

At these words Woody appeared momentarily startled but Mrs Maddison didn't notice. She was already back in the past, reminiscing.

'It was even more beautiful fifty years ago. That's when I met the man of my dreams. I was a journalist, you see, and went over there to report on that tiny country no one knew anything about. It took me three days to get there. No planes back then. Only boats. Ni'juk was my contact, my guide, and I knew as soon as he first took both my hands in his…' Mrs Maddison reached for Woody's hands and held both of his as she spoke. '…and moved them around in the little circle, which as you know is the way they greet people, I just knew… knew we would be together for ever.' Mrs Maddison sighed, a look of contentment on her tired features.

'A happy ending.' Woody's smile brightened, although Lorelai couldn't help but notice the smile didn't quite reach his eyes. She'd always known there was far more to Woody than met the eye and here was her proof. The question was, did she really want to find out what lay beneath all his layers?

CHAPTER THREE

FOR the next two nights in a row, Lorelai dreamt about Woody. Every morning she'd wake up, feeling so at peace, so relaxed, and then as she lay in bed, trying to remember what she'd been dreaming about, it would all come flooding back in one great, big embarrassing rush.

In her dreams he would tenderly take her hand in his, he would caress her skin, he would smile at her in that way that instantly made her knees go weak. He'd draw her closer, brushing the backs of his fingers over her cheeks. He'd look down into her upturned face.

'Relax,' he'd whisper, then he'd press butterfly kisses to her cheeks, then her neck, giving her goose-bumps as he worked his way around to her collar bone. He'd lift his head, brush his thumb over her plump, parted lips before finally giving in to what they both wanted—and boy, oh, boy, did she want it.

'Stop it.' Lorelai opened her eyes and threw back the bed-covers, needing to be busy in order to control her wayward thoughts. Even during morning clinic she'd found herself daydreaming about what it would be like to feel his arms about her, her body pressed against his, the warmth between them building so high it was only right to let off steam.

She could no longer deny she was attracted to him.

The other day when they'd stared at each other out-side Mrs Maddison's house had been a clear give-away that...something was brewing between them. Of course, that didn't mean they had to act on it but even admit-ting to herself that she found Woody to be incredibly sexy was enough to rock her world.

Then again, acknowledging this physical desire she held towards him might be a good thing. It was all right for her to look, to appreciate the facts before her—namely that Woody Moon-Pie was an extremely hand-some man. A physical attraction was something she could control. Now, if she developed *emotional* feelings towards him, well, then she'd be in real big trouble, but a physical attraction was easier to fight.

She'd been physically attracted to John and look where that marriage had ended up. She'd often wished she'd had better self-control, better judgement, bet-ter patience because if she had, perhaps her marriage to John would never have taken place. Although if it hadn't, she wouldn't have Hannah and that little girl had brought so much happiness and meaning into her life, there was no way she'd ever be without her.

Admitting she was attracted to Woody was one thing, following through on that attraction was a completely different matter and she had no intention of following through. He was in town for such a short period of time and then he'd return to his own life.

'Lore?' The door to her consulting room burst open and Ginny stood in the doorway, face flushed, tone ur-gent. 'Emergency. Treatment room. *Now!*'

Lorelai was up and out of her chair before the other woman had even finished talking. She rounded the desk and stalked across the room. 'Status?' She rushed to-

wards the treatment room which was a room specifi-
cally set up to deal with emergencies such as this.

'Five-year-old boy. Not breathing. Face muscles
swollen.'

'Sounds like an allergic reaction. Get Woody.' Lorelai
entered the treatment room to find Woody pulling on a
pair of gloves as the little boy's father placed his non-
breathing child on the examination bed.

'Ritchie? I'm Woody.' He looked into the face of
the terrified child as Lorelai came into the room. She
grabbed a pair of gloves as Ginny ushered the parents
to the side of the room, keeping them out of the way.
'This is Lorelai.' He smiled at the boy, his tone calm
and controlled. 'We're going to take good care of you,'
he said reassuringly.

'What happened?' Lorelai asked as both she and
Woody assessed the situation, taking Ritchie's vital
signs.

'Uh…we were at the club,' the father said hesitantly.

'Eating? At the Oodnaminaby tavern?' Woody confirmed.

'Y-yes.'

'He was eating his food and playing around,' the
mother added. 'And…and swinging on his chair. And
I…I got cross with him and, oh…oh…' She broke down
and started to cry.

'What was he eating?' Woody asked, and glanced
across at Lorelai, their gazes meeting for one split second, but during that brief moment it was clear they were
both on the same page, their hands working completely
in sync as they assessed and made judgements.

Woody was reaching for equipment just as it was on
the tip of Lorelai's tongue to suggest it.

'We thought he was…choking…' the father continued as he consoled his wife.

'Not choking,' Lorelai supplied.

'Allergic reaction,' Woody finished.

'Angio-oedema around the mouth, pulse is dropping, bronchioles narrowing,' Lorelai continued. 'What was he eating?' She glanced over at the parents, the father blinking a few times as though trying to remember.

'Uh…nothing new. He had um…pasta with, uh… cheese. It came in a creamy sauce and he really liked it but he's eaten that sort of thing at home tons of times and this has *never* happened befo—'

'Did you order the adult portion? Not the pasta from the children's menu?' Lorelai asked.

The father frowned. 'Uh…yeah. How did you know?'

Woody already had the EpiPen in his hand, ready to administer the subcutaneous dose of adrenaline that would relieve the immediate threat of Ritchie going into anaphylactic shock.

'My guess is nuts. Spiros, he's the chef at the tavern, puts pine-nuts in the adult serving of creamy pasta. It's not in any of the children's menus.' She directed her comments to Woody but then glanced at the parents once more. 'Is Ritchie allergic to nuts?'

Woody administered the dose and within a matter of seconds the swelling surrounding Ritchie's airways started to decrease and he was no longer gasping for air.

The mother frowned. 'Not that we know. He doesn't usually eat much. Just pasta with cheese and breakfast cereal. We've taken him to a few nutritionists and they say that—'

'So he's never had anything nutty before?'

'Uh…no. Not that I know.' The mother's tone broke

on her last few words and she started to sob against her husband's chest.

'Ginny, call the—'

'On it,' Ginny replied, and pulled her mobile phone from her pocket, calling to Tumut for an ambulance, knowing the practice's emergency procedures back to front.

'We want Ritchie to spend the night in Tumut hospital. It's just a precaution as he needs to be monitored for the next twenty-four hours,' Lorelai continued.

'Hospital? But we…we're supposed to be having ski lessons tomorrow,' the father said, and Lorelai felt her shackles begin to rise at the comment.

'Ski lessons?' Her tone was filled with stunned amazement. She looked at Woody and was surprised when she saw complete compassion for the parents reflected in his eyes. They also seemed to be calming *her* down and where she'd been about to deliver her speech about parents who didn't put the health of their children above their holiday activities, she stopped. Woody gave her a small smile before facing the parents.

'I'm sure if you call the place where you've booked your lessons, they'll be able to accommodate your change in plans. It's certainly a very stressful time for a parent, seeing their children like this…' He pointed to where Lorelai had covered Ritchie with a blanket in order to keep him warm and was hooking her stethoscope into her ears in order to check his breathing.

'Is this the first vacation you've had in a while?' he asked Ritchie's father, who nodded mutely. 'Then congratulations on finding the time to head off on holidays with your family. Sometimes it's not easy to leave the office.'

'No.'

'When did you arrive in the district?'

'Last night.'

'Where have you travelled from?'

'Melbourne.'

Woody smiled. 'That's a lovely city.'

As he continued to speak to the parents, reassuring them and putting them at ease, Lorelai continued to monitor Ritchie, who was responding exceptionally well to the treatment. As Woody talked, she listened to that deep, soothing tone of his, relaxing and charming both mother and father so that when the ambulance arrived from Tumut, the entire family not only understood what was going to happen throughout the next twenty-four hours but somehow seemed closer as a family.

'How did you do that?' Lorelai asked as they stood outside the clinic, watching as the ambulance pulled away. Ritchie and his mother were safely ensconced in the ambulance, his father following behind in the car. The paramedics had turned the siren on for Ritchie's amusement as they drove away from town but had told him that as this wasn't an emergency transfer, they'd have to turn off the lights and siren when they reached the main road. Ritchie was more than happy with that.

'Do what?' Woody asked as he spread his arms wide and breathed in the fresh, crisp, wintry air, enjoying himself. They were at the bottom of the steps that led up to a colonnade where the small row of five businesses was situated—a doctor's surgery, a general store, a take-away, a post-office with banking facilities and a ski-hire and tackle shop. It was the hub of the bustling town that was Oodnaminaby, and Woody liked it. His sister had told him years ago that the town was a lovely place to live and he had to admit that being back here had felt akin to coming home.

It was an odd sensation given he'd never really had a proper home throughout his life. He looked at Lorelai, wondering what she was talking about, admiring the way the pale pink jumper she wore highlighted the blueness of her eyes. Her blonde hair was pulled back low on her neck with a rhinestone clip and he had to admit there was a certain classic style to her that was drawing him in. She was an incredibly beautiful woman and ever since he'd been back in town he'd found himself wanting to spend more time with her, wanting to get to know not only her but her daughter much better. For a man who usually tried to keep to the fringes of the places he worked at, it was a new and confusing sensation.

'Put people at ease so…easily.' She laughed as she tripped over her own words, the sound washing over him with delight. 'It doesn't matter whether it's a young child or a senior citizen, you seem to look right into their souls and you're able to relax them with a simple smile.' She shook her head.

Woody shrugged. 'I'm not sure I know what you're talking about. I'm just me.'

Lorelai rubbed her arms, pleased she'd worn her cashmere jumper and trousers today. It was silly to stand out in the wintry weather but for a moment she didn't feel like going back inside, even though there were patients waiting for both of them.

'You are, aren't you? Just you. Mr Relaxed. Mr Calm. Mr Easy Come, Easy Go.'

Woody's brow puckered for a moment but he smiled. 'I'm still not sure what you're talking about but I think it's a compliment so I'm going to say—thank you, Lore.'

Lorelai couldn't help the gasp that escaped her lips as they stood there in the cold, simply looking at each other. Woody's smile touched his eyes, making them twinkle. It was the way she'd dreamed about him looking at her, the exact image she'd been able to clearly recall that very morning. Of course, in her dream he'd stepped forward and reached for her hand before tugging her close and bringing his mouth agonisingly slowly to meet her own.

She licked her lips and swallowed over the sudden dryness in her throat. Woody's gaze flicked to encompass the action and she watched as the twinkle began to dim from his blue eyes, to be replaced with the hint of repressed desire. The atmosphere around them began to thicken and for a brief moment it was as though they were caught in their own little bubble in time.

The cold was forgotten. The patients inside the waiting room were forgotten. Nothing mattered except the way they made each other feel. It was odd and thrilling and strange and exciting all at the same time.

He breathed out, slowly and a little unsteadily, as though he was trying to hang onto his control. Part of her wanted him to let go, to unleash the tension she could feel emanating from him, to disregard their self-control and see where this moment might take them. The other part of her—the sane part—wanted to turn and run away, to put as much distance between herself and this man who was starting to really infiltrate her life.

Woody swallowed and her gaze followed the action before flicking to his eyes and then to his lips. Her heart was already starting to hammer wildly against her chest but when he took the smallest step towards her, it picked up its already frantic pace. Lorelai kept her gaze trained on his, her eyes wide as he tenderly reached for her hand. The touch of his warm skin on her cooling fingertips flooded her body with the sweetest tingles. She licked her lips again, unable to believe the same scene she'd dreamed about last night was actually playing out for real. If things continued on this path, it would mean that very soon Woody's lips would be pressed against hers. Was that what she wanted? She wasn't sure because right at this moment she didn't seem capable of coherent thought.

'Lore?'

As she continued to look into his eyes, she could see the same confusion and deep attraction she was also experiencing. It was the same way she'd felt when she'd first been introduced to him all those years ago and since that moment she'd felt this way towards him on several occasions. No wonder it was becoming increasingly difficult for her to control her thoughts and dreams where he was concerned. When he looked at her like this, as though she were the most beautiful, most intelligent, most cherished woman on the face of this earth, she had no idea how to respond.

As he rubbed his warm thumb and fingers over hers, her breathlessness seemed to increase. She licked her lips again and shook her head ever so slightly. 'Woody, I don't...' She couldn't finish the sentence as he edged even closer, the warmth from his body now surrounding her as the cool air puffed from her mouth, their little steam clouds mixing and blending in the air.

The tinkling of the bell above the practice door broke through their bubble, popping it instantly.

'There you two are.' Ginny called from the top of the steps. The instant they heard her voice, both of them stepped back, the moment dissipating along with the coolness from their breath. 'What are you doing out here?'

Lorelai tore her gaze from Woody's and headed up the steps. 'Nothing. Coming in now. Gee, it really is cold out here.'

'What? You're only just realising that?' Ginny asked, raising her eyebrows with interest. Lorelai ignored the comment. 'Anyway,' Ginny continued, 'Woody, there's a phone call for you. It's Pacific Medical Aid.'

Woody headed up the steps after Lorelai, a deep frown creasing his brow. He straightened his shoulders, as though a little uncomfortable, before pulling his mobile phone from his pocket and checking the display. Five missed calls, all from PMA. 'My phone must have been out of range.'

'It happens a lot here. Just was well they knew how to track you down. I'll put the call through to your clinic room,' Ginny said as the three of them headed inside. Lorelai watched Woody closely, noting the change in his posture, a slightly defensive stance. Did calls from PMA mean he'd be leaving Oodnaminaby sooner rather than later? Whatever it was, she hoped everything was all right because he didn't look all that happy.

Lorelai picked up a set of case notes from the desk and looked at the backlog of patients waiting for her due to the emergency. 'Plency.' She smiled at her patient. 'Come on through,' she said, and waited while the mother of four gathered up her children and shepherded them and herself through to Lorelai's clinic room. As Lorelai walked past Woody's room, the consulting-room door was closed and she could hear his deep, muted tones as he spoke on the phone.

At the back of her mind was the thought he might have to leave them sooner rather than later and while she'd been almost counting down the days until Honey and Edward returned so Woody could leave and her life could return to its normal pace, the sudden thought that he might need to leave sooner filled her with a sense of deep sadness mixed with a healthy dose of regret.

Throughout the rest of the day Lorelai only caught the faintest glimpses of Woody as they caught up on their patient lists. When she did pass him in the corridor, he would smile or nod politely as he continued with his work. Lorelai scanned his face for signs of stress or concern from the call from PMA but found nothing.

After the day was done and with Ginny having to leave early, Lorelai went into the kitchenette to tidy up and switch off the urn so everything was ready for tomorrow.

'Did you manage to catch up?' Woody's deep voice startled her and a cup she was drying slipped from her hands. Juggling it a bit, she managed to catch it. 'Sorry.' He smiled sheepishly. 'Didn't mean to startle you.'

'Uh…yes. I managed to catch up on my patient list. How about you?'

'Just, but only because Mr Sommerton cancelled.'

Lorelai raised her eyebrows. 'Mr Sommerton cancelled?'

'You seem surprised.'

She shrugged and continued putting the cups away. Woody walked over to the sink, picked up the cloth and started wiping the table as they talked. It was thoughtful and useful, exactly what one of the Goldmark men would have done. She knew she'd entered her marriage with rose-coloured glasses, expecting all men to be the same as those she'd been raised with, which was why she'd received such a shock to find that deep down inside John had been nothing like the men she knew. Woody, however, was showing her that she shouldn't tar every man with the same brush as John. He was a good man, a man of principle and honour, that much was evident simply from his actions. The knowledge warmed her heart, which was exactly what she didn't want. Glancing at him now, she could still feel the tingles where he'd touched her hand earlier in the day, and combined with the dreams and the way he seemed to be infiltrating every part of her life, she'd have to be stronger with the barriers she was almost desperate to erect.

'What's wrong?' Woody asked.

'Huh?'

'You're frowning.'

'I am?' Lorelai raised a hand to her forehead to check and realised he was right. 'Oh, I…uh…was just thinking we should add Mr Sommerton to the house-call list. He's a stickler for keeping his appointments so it might be best to check there isn't anything wrong that stopped him from coming today. The Jindabyne clinic is doing house calls this week so I'll make sure to call them in the morning.'

'You really care about your patients,' he stated. 'I like that.'

'That's what this practice is about.'

He nodded. 'That's how most of the PMA staff are. They're people who don't practise medicine for the money but for how they can be of service to others.' He returned the cloth to the sink and gave the area a final wipe before walking towards the door.

Now that he'd opened the conversation, Lorelai took the opportunity to make sure there were no drastic repercussions from his earlier phone call. 'By the way, is everything OK? With PMA, I mean.' When he gave her a blank look, she continued. 'The phone call you received earlier in the day?'

A guarded look entered his eyes. 'Oh, that. Yes. Everything's…fine.'

'You don't sound too sure.'

'Everything's fine.' The words came out a little too quickly and Lorelai was startled at his reaction. She hadn't meant to pry or to make him feel uncomfortable. 'They just had some questions regarding a village in Tarparnii,' he continued after a momentary pause, as though he was collecting his thoughts, deciding what to say and what to conceal. 'There were some things that required…clarification.'

'Oh. OK, then.' She forced a smile and nodded, even though she didn't understand at all. What she *did* know was that this room was starting to feel smaller, the two of them here, after hours, the clinic empty. She would have headed out but Woody blocked the doorway with his tall frame.

'I just thought you might have been called back into the field sooner rather than later, that's all.'

'No.' He shook his head for emphasis. 'I've told everyone that I'm here until my sister has had enough of travelling. This is the last opportunity she and Edward will have to be together, to see some new sights before the baby is born, and I'm going to support her in any way I can.' There was an edge, a vehemence to his words, as though he wasn't just saying this to her but to someone else. Perhaps it was the person who had called him earlier. 'I won't be leaving you in the lurch, Lorelai.'

There it was again, the hint of angry determination, as though he needed her to believe him.

'I never thought you would.'

He straightened his shoulders and exhaled slowly. 'I'm a man of my word.'

'Understood.'

'Good.' With a brisk nod, he turned on his heel and stalked from the room, leaving her standing there wondering what on earth had just happened.

That night, as Woody made himself some dinner, Honey and Edward's large home seemed even quieter than usual. He ate his dinner in silence, took a shower and then prowled around the different rooms, looking at the photographs on the walls, the Goldmark family portraits, the pictures Honey had added when she'd married Edward almost three years ago. His sister was happy. She'd found the place where she belonged, which was great for Honey as she'd been searching for so long.

But what about him? At the moment he felt so…disjointed and he'd never felt that way before.

He looked at the picture of himself, Honey, their parents and grandparents, which sat on the bookshelf. It had been taken at Honey's wedding—his whole family. It had been a good day. Throughout his childhood he'd been able to accept his parents for who they were, largely because Honey had been the one providing him with a stable influence. When he'd finished medical school and started his surgical rotation, he'd had the stable influence of hospital hierarchy to guide him. Even when he'd headed overseas to work in Tarparnii, he'd been governed by the rules and regulations set out by Pacific Medical Aid as well as the Tarparniian culture.

He'd met a wonderful woman, he'd married her, had had a child and for a brief time his life had felt complete. Then it had all been ripped apart, taken from him in a dramatic way, and at the time he hadn't thought he'd ever be able to move forward.

Woody walked to his satchel, which he'd left by the

back door when he'd arrived home. He took out his laptop and switched it on, re-reading the emails sent from his mother-in-law, Nilly, via PMA. It was the only way she was able to contact him, to send information and updates on the village he'd previously called his home.

He hadn't replied to the emails because he'd simply been looking for a bit of time out. The pressures that had been placed on his shoulders after the tragedy that had struck his life had been something he'd never expected. For four years he'd carried the burden and he'd done it willingly, not wanting to let even more people down. Then today, because he hadn't answered his emails, PMA had tracked him down at the Oodnaminaby clinic, calling him with news that he'd need to return to his village for the *par'Mach* festival.

Woody closed the lid to his laptop and shut his eyes. Leaning back in his chair, he pushed his hands through his hair. After the tragedy he'd known what was expected of him and he'd carried that burden willingly. Yet somehow things had become incredibly complicated. His life had been calm, comfortable and controlled, and now he wasn't sure which way was up.

And it was all Lorelai's fault.

If only he'd been able to say no to Honey when she'd asked him to come and locum for her while she had a bit of a holiday, but he hadn't been able to. Honey had *always* been there for him throughout his entire life and he would always appreciate that. She was his sister. He'd known before he'd even set foot in Ood that being around Lorelai would be difficult. He'd often thought about her, often thought about that night when her husband had died and he'd watched over her and Hannah with infinite care. He'd felt her pain and he'd understood her loss. Support was what she'd needed and he'd done his best to provide it, but sitting there in a chair, holding her tiny baby girl in his arms as he'd watched Lorelai sleeping, her blonde hair splayed out over the pillow-case, her pretty features relaxed and at peace, Woody had felt such a deep stirring of emotion, of attachment, of need and longing that as soon as Honey had arrived the next morning, he'd hightailed it out of town.

Perhaps he'd overreacted. Perhaps leaving town so suddenly hadn't been the right decision to make, but in admitting to himself he'd had feelings for Lorelai he'd also realised he was emotionally ready to move forward with his life. After Kalenia's death, he'd never thought he'd ever be so deeply attracted to a woman again… and then he'd met Lorelai.

Since he'd returned to Oodnaminaby, he'd realised the sensations he'd felt towards Lorelai three years ago were still alive and kicking, and given the staring com-petitions they'd been having lately, the way their eyes seemed to meet and hold, both of them caught in such powerful sensations, the only natural course of action was to close the distance between them and press their mouths together in total surrender.

Woody closed his eyes as he relived the moment again, staring at her and having her look back at him as though she had been on the same page. The attrac-tion between them was clear and he wished he could let nature take its course, but he couldn't.

He wasn't a free man. His own wants and desires needed to be shelved, to be put aside in favour of pro-tecting others. Nilly was expecting an answer and rightly so. The *par'Mach* festival was a big deal, espe-cially for his sisters-in-law and as head of the clan, his presence was required. As head of the clan, he would do his duty. As head of the clan, he would deny himself the happiness being around Lorelai afforded him.

His life wasn't here in Ood and it would be wrong of him to lead her on. He should pull back, put some distance between himself and Lorelai even though it was the last thing he wanted to do.

CHAPTER FOUR

THE following week, Lorelai was finishing up her clinic for the day when Ginny came in with a message.

'It's Martha. She's worried about Aidan. She thought he might have had a cold but last night he started vomiting and he's also had diarrhoea. She was going to take him to Tumut hospital but now, when she tries to move him, he says he's in too much pain. Her husband's out working at the ski resort and has both sets of snow chains in his car. She wanted to know if she should call the ambulance to her place or whether you wanted to come out and see him. Also, given the snowfall they had last night, she can't get a babysitter and all her kids are home.' Ginny looked up from the piece of paper she held in her hand where she'd quickly scribbled down some notes. 'So? What do you want to do?'

Lorelai thought for a moment. 'I think it's best if I head out to take a look. There has been a lot of bad gastro going around and chances are Aidan might actually feel better by tomorrow morning. I was on the phone to Tumut hospital earlier today and they said they've had a swag of admissions and the ambulances have been really busy. They've even airlifted two cases to Wagga Wagga Base hospital for further surgical treatment and one person was sent to Canberra for surgical intervention.'

'Well, Tumut is only a small thirty-four-bed hospital with a small operating theatre and no resident surgeon. They can't be expected to deal with mass emergencies,' Ginny rationalised. 'I'll call Martha back and tell her you'll head out.'

'I think that's the best alternative. The weather report said we'll be getting more snow this evening so the sooner I leave the better.' Lorelai checked the clock as she spoke. 'I'll pick up Hannah and take her with me. She can play with Martha's brood while I see to Aidan.'

'Do you think it might be appendicitis?' Ginny asked. 'She said it doesn't matter where she presses on his stomach, he says it hurts all over.'

Lorelai thought for a moment. 'There's a high possibility it could be that.'

'In that case, why not take me with you?' A deep voice spoke from the doorway and both women turned to see Woody lounging against the doorjamb.

Lorelai's breath caught and she fumbled with the papers in her hand, dropping her prescription pad and knocking over her coffee cup. Thankfully, it was empty. She quickly righted everything, looking down at her hands, willing them to obey the commands coming from her brain. Even just one brief glance at him had her all flustered. Though there'd been no repeat of their almost kiss of the previous week, that didn't mean her dreams hadn't been filled with images of her and Woody, kissing, touching and more. She'd made a vow to avoid him. Distance was definitely the only way to go.

'I couldn't help but overhear what Ginny was saying. How old is Aidan?'

'Uh…' Lorelai's mind was blank. Details? How was she supposed to recall details when his closeness turned her mind to mush?

'He's seventeen,' Ginny provided. 'He's Martha's eldest boy. She has seven children altogether, the youngest has just turned five.'

'Well if he's been having bad stomach pains, vomiting and diarrhoea then *I'm* your best bet. It might simply be a bad case of gastroenteritis but if it's not, if it's something more serious, it would be best if I came with you.' He nodded for emphasis. 'If the patient can't come to the general surgeon then, by golly, we'll take the general surgeon to the patient!' Woody thrust his arm triumphantly into the air as he spoke and Lorelai couldn't help but smile at his antics. He was handsome, clever and funny. If she had to pick any man to have a crush on, she was right to choose him. Then again, every woman in town had a crush on him so she guessed that made her normal and in no danger of taking those feelings further…except in her dreams.

'I'll go pack a medical bag with things I might need,' he finished before she could say another word, and disappeared as quickly and as quietly as he'd arrived.

'I guess that's it, then,' Ginny remarked, coming over to remove Lorelai's coffee cup from her desk. 'Go and get Hannah. I'll tidy up here while you go off gallivanting with the handsome surgeon.'

'I'm hardly gallivanting, Ginny. Besides, Woody is right. He would be Aidan's best bet. He doesn't know the way to Martha's farm otherwise he could go on his own. This is just a medical callout. Nothing more.'

Ginny grinned broadly and nodded. 'Sure. Of course it is.'

'Then why do you sound as though you don't believe me?'

'Oh, I do, darl, and I can see that you're not at all excited about spending some time stuck in the intimate confines of the car with Woody.'

'What? What are you talking about?' Lorelai fumbled with the paperwork in her hands once more. Ginny raised an eyebrow.

'You're not usually this flustered, Lorelai Rainbow. There's something going on between you two, don't forget I saw the way you two were standing outside last week—the heat could've melted all that fresh snow!'

'Shh.' Lorelai rushed around the desk and put her finger across Ginny's lips. The other woman stopped talking but smiled knowingly. Lorelai looked cautiously down the corridor, hoping Woody hadn't overheard them.

'It's about time you became interested in another man,' Ginny whispered when Lorelai had removed her hand. 'You couldn't do better. He's a lovely lad.'

Lorelai sighed and shook her head. 'He's about as stable as…as a three-legged chair!' She returned to her desk and gathered her haphazard bundle of papers together before thrusting them into her bag. 'So don't go thinking you can play matchmaker, all right?' She collected her keys. 'I just can't afford to make another mistake. I have Hannah to consider. *If* I ever decided to become involved with another man, or even marry again, it will be to someone who's going to be there for me, for Hannah—all the time. Not someone who spends their life gallivanting around overseas.'

'Woody does a lot of good with his overseas work.'

'And I'm not denying that and nor am I wanting him to give it up. I simply need someone I can depend upon.'

'Someone like Simon Arlington?' Ginny suggested. 'He's been sweet on you for years. Even before you married John.'

Lorelai didn't say anything but a frown marred her brow as she thought about Simon. He was a shy but sweet man, six years older than her, and had been working in the Jindabyne medical practice for the past seven years. Although they'd worked together on occasions, it was only recently that he'd asked her out in a social capacity. They'd had three dates over a period of six months and whilst they'd been nice, Lorelai had to confess he didn't set her heart aflame. All she needed was one second in Woody's company and she was a blazing inferno of rioting hormones!

'He's due back at the Jindabyne clinic next week, isn't he?' Ginny continued.

'Yes.'

'Such a nice man to rush home to Perth and care for his ailing mother. It's what every parent wants. Dependable children, and he'll make a dependable partner if that's what you're looking for. It's been…what? Three months since you last saw him?'

'Yes.' Lorelai put on her coat and scarf before wriggling her fingers into her gloves and reaching for her bag and keys.

'Have you been pining for him at all?'

Lorelai glared at Ginny. 'I know what you're trying to do.'

'And what's that, lovey?'

'To point out that as I haven't appeared to miss Simon, I can't really be all that interested in him.' Lorelai walked around her desk and stood in front of Ginny, leaning over to kiss the woman's cheek, her tone calm and controlled. 'I need to focus on Hannah, on doing what's best for her future.'

'What about yours?' Ginny asked quietly, and placed her hand on Lorelai's cheek. 'You deserve a world of happiness after everything you've been through. If Simon Arlington is the man to make you happy for the rest of your life, then that's wonderful, darl, but I see the way you look at Woody and I see the way Woody looks at you.'

'Woody looks at me? How? What do you mean?' The calmness momentarily disappeared.

Ginny's answer was to laugh and shake her head. 'Oh, you're definitely *not* interested in him. I can see that.'

Lorelai closed her eyes for a moment, collecting her thoughts and pulling herself together. 'I know you only have my best interests at heart.' She sighed and opened her eyes, determined to remain calm and controlled. 'Hannah is more important to me than my own love life. If providing a stable and happy environment for her means I deny myself a love life, then so be it. Hannah comes first.'

Ginny nodded. 'You're probably right, darl. Now, off with you.'

'Yes. Right.' Lorelai dug around in her coat pocket for her car keys. 'Would you mind calling Connie and tell her I'll be there directly to collect Hannah, please? Then I'll come back and pick up Woody.'

'Right you are, lovey.'

As Lorelai walked to the car, she thought on Ginny's words, realising she hadn't thought much about Simon while he'd been gone. In fact, she rarely thought about him when he was in the district. She shook her head as she drove the short distance to Connie's house.

During their three sporadic dates, Simon's behaviour had been exemplary and he'd never even made an attempt to kiss her. He would call her every few months, receive an update on the status of the Oodnaminaby clinic, give her an update on the Jindabyne side of things and ask after Hannah. Ginny was right. Simon was a nice, dependable man and he deserved better than her less than lukewarm attention.

'How much longer do you need to be away, Honey?' she muttered to herself as she headed up Connie's front path, being careful not to slip on the wet ground. She would just have to put up with Woody creating havoc within her life for a while longer. Then he would leave and she could find the neat, ordered, calm world that, up until two weeks ago, had been her life.

Within the hour, Lorelai was making her way out to Martha's place, which was situated on a farm between Oodnaminaby and the old village of Kiandra. The roads hadn't been too wet, the four-wheel-drive making short work of any slippery patches, and just before they'd turned off the main road, taking the gravel track that led to the family farm, Woody had volunteered to put the snow chains onto the tyres.

'You and Hannah stay nice and warm inside the car,' he'd instructed. 'Won't take me long.'

Lorelai had always known he was a gentleman from the night when John had died. She'd needed someone strong, someone to lean on, and Woody had been there for her. He'd shown her that chivalry wasn't dead and when he did little things like offering to put on the snow chains, it made her realise just how much she missed having someone to rely on.

'It's the little things that make the biggest difference,' her father always said, and Woody was proving him right. He'd shovelled the walk at Mrs Maddison's house, he'd put the chains on her tyres and when they arrived at Martha's house just as the sun was disappearing from the sky and snow covering the front garden, Woody collected Hannah from her car seat and carried her on his shoulders into the house, making the little girl giggle with delight. The sound warmed her heart and pierced it, all at the same time.

As soon as Lorelai entered the house, she carried the medical kit through to Aidan's bedroom, where the teenager was lying, curled up in his blankets. Woody was hard on her heels. 'I've left Hannah playing with Martha's children. She'll be fine with them.'

'Thanks,' Lorelai replied as she opened the bag and removed the stethoscope, noting that Woody seemed to genuinely care for her daughter, ensuring the child was safe.

Woody put his hand on the boy's forehead. 'He's burning up. Aidan? I'm Woody and of course you know Lorelai. We're here to help.'

'Pulse rate is elevated. Gurgling sounds in the abdomen. It's very tight and slightly distended. Just as well you packed a drip.'

'From what Ginny told me of the phone call, I came prepared for emergency surgery.' He pulled the equipment he needed from the bag as Lorelai asked a hovering Martha for a bowl of cool water and a face washer. 'The best way to lower Aidan's temperature is to sponge him down.' At his words, the anxious mother immediately headed off to do his bidding.

'This is definitely not gastro.' Lorelai said, happy and relieved Woody had decided to accompany her. If he hadn't, she'd be trying to figure out the best way to transport Aidan to Wagga Wagga Base hospital, which was the main hospital for rural surgical cases. She would have had to organise a plane or helicopter to come to the property to transfer the teenager but in this weather they wouldn't have been able to fly. Having Woody here, a trained general surgeon with all the equipment he needed, was Aidan's best chance of survival.

'I love teenagers who hang things from their ceilings.' Woody reached up and took down a large skull and crossbones home-made mobile Aidan had had floating around on his ceiling and looped the end of the bag of saline through the hook in the ceiling. 'Once, in Tarparnii, I was forced to operate in the middle of a jungle. I was literally surrounded by scrub and trees, the patient lying on a bed of dead leaves and twigs,' he related, and for a split second Lorelai wasn't sure whether he was talking to Aidan, trying to keep him alert, or to her. Either way, she was very interested in what he had to say.

'There was absolutely nowhere for me to hang a drip so I quickly lashed together a few sticks with a vine and stuck it in the ground, like a very tall cross. It wasn't all that strong and I was sure the twigs were going to break but thankfully they held long enough. I was able to repair the patient's large abdominal slash and suture him closed just as the twigs finally snapped. Thankfully by then help had arrived and we were able to move the patient back to a more sterile location.'

'Sounds so…full on,' Lorelai remarked as she drew up an injection of an anti-emetic to stop Aidan's vomiting.

'Hang in there, Aidan.' Woody finished inserting the drip and accepted the bowl of cold water from Martha, beckoning her into the room. 'Can you start cooling him down? Wipe his forehead, his face, around his neck. I need to gently feel his abdomen and then we can give him a mild anaesthetic.'

'What?' Martha was aghast but she continued to wipe her son down. 'What do you mean, anaesthetic? Isn't the ambulan—?'

'There's no time,' Lorelai interjected.

'I'm a general surgeon, Martha,' Woody reassured her. 'I've seen these symptoms so often, I know them by heart. Aidan has appendicitis and the sooner we remove it, the healthier he'll be. It won't be a full anaesthetic,' he continued as he carefully palpated Aidan's abdomen, both Lorelai and Martha wincing when the boy cried out in terrified pain. 'Symptoms are clear. Do you concur, Lore?'

'I do.'

'Good. Let's get started.' Woody reached into the medical bag and withdrew a vial and syringe.

'Midazolam?' Lorelai queried.

'By far the best option in this scenario. It's safe, easy to use, gives us enough time to operate and means Aidan doesn't need to recover from a general anaesthetic as well as everything else that's happened to him.' Woody quickly calculated the dose Aidan would require before administering it. It wasn't long before Aidan's face relaxed as he slipped into oblivion.

'Thanks, Martha.' Woody took the face washer from her then held both her hands in his and looked into her eyes. 'Would you mind getting some clean sheets for Aidan's bed and two large towels? I'll also need a bowl of warm soapy water in about half an hour's time.'

Lorelai watched as Martha nodded, responding to Woody's calm, controlled voice.

'Aidan's going to be just fine. In a few days he'll be

back to his normal teenage self.' With a reassuring smile Woody let go of Martha's hands and the woman headed out of the room to do his bidding. Then he turned to Lorelai. 'Where's the bathroom? We need to scrub.'

They took it in turns to scrub their hands and by the time Lorelai returned and pulled on a pair of gloves and disposable apron Woody had packed into the bag, he'd already sterilised and draped Aidan's abdomen. A tall lamp, which ordinarily stood over Aidan's study desk, was shining brightly on the area, ready for operating.

'How are you feeling?' he asked Lorelai. 'Nervous? Worried? Calm?'

She shrugged her shoulders. 'Aidan requires an immediate appendectomy to avoid peritonitis,' she stated. 'I'm just glad you're here to do it.'

'Hmm, is that confidence in my ability or relief I hear in your voice?' he asked, taking the scalpel from its sterile packet. Lorelai looked at the instruments he'd set out on a sterile cloth on top of Aidan's desk and picked up the swabs, ready to assist him.

'Both.'

With a quick smile that almost made her knees buckle, Woody nodded. 'Then, Dr Rainbow, let us begin.' His incision was neat and precise and it was clear as his clever fingers worked that he really had performed this surgery many times before.

'I became so used to doing appendectomies via laparotomy that when I returned to a large teaching hospital I almost had to retrain myself to do it laparoscopically,' he remarked as he began suturing the layers closed.

Aidan's fever had broken and Lorelai had added a course of IV antibiotics to his drip to help guard against infection. She continued to watch Woody, her respect for his skill having increased rapidly during the past twenty minutes.

'Tarparnii seems to be a very special, very personal place for you, Woody.' Her words were clear yet soft and when his gaze flicked up to meet hers, she wasn't sure whether he was warning her the topic was off limits or whether he was surprised at her astute comment.

'It is and always will be.'

'Not that I'm wanting to pry…' she began, and was rewarded with a rich deep chuckle. 'What?' She stopped her flow of conversation.

'Nothing. It's just that any time a woman says "I'm not wanting to pry", it means they're *about* to pry.' Woody laughed again and reached for the prepared bandage, fixing it in place. A moment later he stepped back from Aidan's bed and pulled off his gloves and apron, balling them up and stowing them in a garbage bag. Lorelai followed suit and as they tidied up, he said calmly, 'If you want to know about my life in Tarparnii, just ask. I'll tell you want you want to know.' He spread his arms wide and almost knocked over the lamp. He switched it off and moved it away from the bed while Lorelai performed Aidan's observations.

She was a little annoyed at him for seeing through her intention and now that he was giving her permission to pry, she found she'd rather not know anything about him. 'It's fine,' she remarked, trying not to show him how huffy she felt. She continued clearing up, continued trying to ignore him, continued telling herself that keeping her distance meant not wanting to know about his past.

'Come on, Lore. Ask what's on your mind,' he cajoled as he moved past her to check the drip, noticing that she shrank away, desperate to ensure their bodies didn't accidentally touch. 'Did I like working and living in Tarparnii?' He asked the question himself. 'Yes. Did I meet people who became incredibly important to me? Yes. Did I fall in love and marry a Tarparnese girl?' His voice dipped as he spoke these last words and Lorelai instantly turned, lifting her gaze to his, surprised but almost desperate to hear his answer.

'Yes.' He paused, his gaze still intent on hers, the two of them caught in this moment in time, nothing else existing but the two of them. 'Did something bad happen to her?' The pain she could see reflected in his eyes was deep. She recognised it because it was pain she'd felt before. 'Yes.' His answer was barely a whisper. 'Do I like to talk about it?'

Lorelai gently shook her head from side to side before answering for him. 'No.'

CHAPTER FIVE

As SHE helped set the table for dinner, Martha insisting the three of them stay the night as it was too wet to head off now, Lorelai found herself watching the way Woody interacted with Hannah. The fact he'd been married, the fact his wife had been cruelly taken from him, made her look at him in a completely different light.

No longer did he seem to be such a drifter but instead a man who was keeping his mind occupied, keeping busy, moving around, doing anything and everything he could to stop his thoughts from dwelling on the pain and agony that went hand in hand with losing a loved one.

Lorelai had been eleven when her mother had passed away and even now, so many years later, there were days when the loss would encompass her so completely she found it difficult to breathe. She missed the wholesome hugs, the tender stroking of her hair, the reassuring smiles.

Thankfully, Edward's mother—Hannah—had happily taken on the role as surrogate mother, drawing Lorelai into the bonds of their family, treating her as her very own.

'I don't have a daughter,' Hannah had whispered a few days after the funeral. They had been sitting on the seat in the lovely garden Hannah had made in her back yard, eleven-year-old Lorelai held securely on her lap as they'd watched a butterfly dance around the flowers. 'And your mother and I were always as close as sisters.' Hannah had tenderly stroked Lorelai's long blonde hair. 'Will you be my girl, Lorelai? We can go shopping in Tumut, we can sit and paint our toenails together, we can talk and talk and laugh at the boys. We can do all those girly things both of us used to do with your mum. What do you think?'

Lorelai remembered putting her arms around Hannah's neck, nodding emphatically before bursting into tears and burying her face against Hannah's neck. She'd never called her 'Mum', always 'Aunty Hannah' but the emotional bond between the two of them had grown rapidly from that day forward. Hannah had saved her, given a young girl the reassurance, the strength and the power to move forward with her life.

Then when Hannah and her husband Cameron had passed away during an avalanche not long after Lorelai's twentieth birthday, the grieving process had started all over again. Edward and his four brothers had grieved alongside her. Lorelai's father, BJ, had held them all together, binding them even closer as a family.

Years later, when she'd met John, Lorelai had yearned for the counsel of her mother or Hannah, desperate to know what she should do. John had been flattering and attentive, always making her feel as though she was truly special. Then, after their marriage, everything had changed. He would argue with her when she questioned him about all the times he didn't come home from the snowfields. He'd twist everything around to imply that it was all her fault, that she was paranoid, imagining things that weren't there. The man who had legally been her husband had ripped her heart out and tossed it carelessly aside.

She'd grieved for John, for the loss of his life. He'd been her husband but from the way Woody had spoken of his wife, it was clear that their marriage had been a loving one. That would have been a terrible tragedy for him to endure. A tragedy to make him keep on moving, keep on being busy so he didn't have to continually face the fact that she was gone. No wonder he'd known exactly what to say and do on the night John had died. *He'd* already been through it, the loss of a spouse.

Now she watched him, sitting on the sofa, a book open in front of him, children all around. They listened attentively as he read them a story, effectively keeping them out of Martha's way whilst she and Steven, the second oldest, continued with the meal preparations. The story he read was one about a mouse who tended to get into mischief, and this particular story was one of her daughter's favourites.

Hannah was sitting on her knees, jiggling with happy excitement as Woody read on. Her little hands clutched her chest in anticipation as Woody neared the end of the story. When he'd finished, Hannah giggled and clapped her hands, clearly delighted with the predicted outcome.

'Yay.' She climbed up onto his lap and put her arms around Woody's neck, hugging him close and pressing a quick kiss to his cheek. 'I lub that story.'

Woody seemed surprised at the action, the innocence of a child's kiss. He raised his hand and brushed his fingers lightly across his cheek before he smiled back at the little girl.

'Thank you for the kiss,' he said, and Lorelai could hear through his rich and honest tone that he really meant it.

Hannah kept her arms about his neck as the other children searched through their bookshelves for another story for Woody to read. Lorelai edged closer so she could hear what else was being said.

'You welcome.' Hannah smiled at him and Woody reached out to stroke his hand over her lovely blonde locks. A lump appeared in Lorelai's throat at his caring action and she quickly tried to swallow over it. 'I weally like that story,' Hannah told him again. 'It's my favouwite.'

'Mine, too,' he agreed. 'Aunty Honey used to read me that story when I was a little boy.'

'Weally?' Hannah's big blue eyes widened in surprise. 'Was you little?'

Woody's smile increased. 'Yes, I was. A very long time ago now, although Aunty Honey and your mother would probably say that I've never bothered to grow up.'

Another book was thrust in his direction and he accepted it with a smile, the children instantly settling down with looks of excited anticipation on their faces as they waited for him to begin.

The way the children so readily, so easily accepted Woody was a clear indication of his true personality. He was an extremely likeable man...a fact she was well aware of. He accommodated the children around him, ensuring everyone could see the pictures before he began reading.

'OK, kids,' Martha called a few minutes later as Lorelai still stood, spellbound by the man before her. 'Your father's home,' Martha continued. 'Which means it's dinnertime.'

A few of the children started to wriggle and complain, not wanting to leave the exciting world Woody was creating as he told the story. He started to read faster and a moment later, before Martha could come in and tell them *all* off, he finished the story.

'Quick.' He stood to his feet. 'You'd better go and wash your hands before your mother tells me off.'

'Nah, she wouldn't do that,' Riley, Martha's middle child said.

'I wouldn't be too sure,' Caitlin, his older sister, retorted as she headed towards the bathroom.

'I want more stories,' Hannah demanded. 'Not dinner.'

Woody picked her up and tapped his finger to her nose. 'Perhaps, if you're very good and eat all your dinner, we might be able to have a few more stories before bedtime.'

A cheer went up from all the children and Hannah quickly wriggled from his arms and raced along with the others to wash her hands in the bathroom. It wasn't until they'd all gone that Woody raised his arms above his head and stretched his cramped muscles. Lorelai watched the action from her vantage point in the shadows, eagerly drinking in the sight of his broad shoulders and firm muscles, her mouth going dry.

The shirt he was wearing rode up a little higher and the waistband of his denim jeans dipped a little lower, revealing a generous amount of rock-hard abdominals. Lorelai's gaze was drawn to the area, a small smattering of dark hair around his navel, his skin more tanned than she'd originally thought. She swallowed over the sudden dryness in her throat and unconsciously licked her lips at the perfect male specimen before her.

'See anything you like?' Woody asked a second later, and Lorelai instantly met his gaze. However, instead of seeing a teasing sort of censure, she received the message of reciprocated interest. He'd been well aware she'd been watching, and he'd clearly enjoyed every moment of her visual caresses. 'Should I turn the other way? Give you a different view?' he continued to tease, lowering his arms and gently twisting from side to side. All the time he was moving, his gaze held hers, and Lorelai couldn't help the blush that tinged her cheeks or the speechlessness that racked her mind.

'It's all right to look, Lore,' he said softly, seeing her discomfort increase. He moved to stand before her, his tone soft and intimate. 'You can even touch if you really want to.' Even though the light on this side of the room was dim, now that he was closer he could see the embarrassment on her beautiful upturned face. 'No need to feel self-conscious, Lore.'

'How can you even say that?' she blurted, quickly lowering her tone lest anyone should hear them. They'd come here to attend a sick teenager, not to flirt with each other.

'Easy. I like it when you look at me, Lorelai, especially when you look at me *like that*. Do you have any idea just how long it's been since I've felt the visual caress of a beautiful woman?'

'Uh...half a day?'

He smiled. 'No, and I'm not saying the women of Oodnaminaby aren't beautiful, just that they're never serious.'

'You are so conceited.'

'No, I'm not. I'm truthful. The last time I felt such a powerful and magnetic caress was about three months after I first met Kalenia.' His words were quiet yet filled with an intenseness that caught her off guard. The man standing before her was the same man who had cared for her on that fateful night. He had been serious yet protective and this time he was also a little flirty. She liked it.

'Kalenia?' Even as she said the foreign name, deep down Lorelai knew what his next words were going to be.

'My wife. I'm not the type of man to play the field, despite what you might think.'

'I don't think that…or at least I don't any more.'

'Thank you.'

'Was Kalenia receptive to your advances?'

Woody chuckled and leaned one hand on the wall behind her. Lorelai breathed in, her senses filled with the essence and scent of him. It was a heady combination, his spicy scent complemented by his warm nearness. She swallowed and tried hard not to lick her suddenly dry lips.

'Actually, no. She resisted my advances at first, telling me there was no way she'd ever marry an Australia *p'tak* like me.' He smiled at the memory. 'She was so clever and smart and pretty and full of life.' A hint of sadness tinged his words. 'Your strength and perseverance, the way you care for your patients and your daughter, your powerful and giving heart…' He nodded. 'You remind me a lot of her. The same inner qualities.'

He reached out and stroked the backs of his fingers down her cheek, leaning in a little closer, their breaths starting to mingle, the heat rising between them. 'Life has an…intriguing way of turning out, don't you think? Here we are, years later, both of us wary and scarred from our first marriages, unsure of ourselves, of protocol, given we've not been interested in anyone else for years, wondering what to do next.'

When he stood this close and spoke so openly, it was all she could do to keep her knees from buckling beneath her due to his enigmatic presence. She forced herself to close her eyes for a moment, just long enough to break the contact, to ensure the strong connection intensifying between them was severed before opening her eyes. The sights, sounds and delicious smells from the house around them started to permeate her mind, bringing her back to normal.

'What do we do next?' she reiterated, finding superhuman strength from somewhere in order to take a small step away from him. He was dangerous and he was definitely threatening her well-ordered life with his charisma, his chivalry and his charm. 'The answer to that question is very easy.'

'It is?'

'Yes. The next thing we do is...go and have some dinner.' With that, Lorelai turned sharply on her heel and walked away from him.

Throughout dinner, with Woody seated directly opposite her, it was difficult *not* to look at him—so she gave up trying to fight it. The fact that he was right in her line of sight wasn't her fault. Although she'd set the table, she hadn't decided where everyone would sit and, besides, she had Hannah beside her, sitting in the special booster seat, feeling very special and satisfied with herself. She ate up all her vegetables and five bites of meat.

'Good girl,' Lorelai praised as Hannah asked to be excused from the table, so she could go and play with the others. 'Not too long,' she told her daughter. 'It'll be bedtime soon.'

'But we don't have our beds,' she rationalised. 'Where we gonna sleep, Mummy?'

'You and I, possum, are going to sleep in the same

bed.' Lorelai pointed to the sofa where Woody had previously been ensconced reading to the children.

'Where's Woody gonna sleep?' Hannah's wide eyes looked at the man who was fast becoming far too special to her.

'I'll be sleeping in Aidan's room,' he told Hannah. 'That way, I can look after Aidan throughout the night.'

'You don't have to do that,' Lorelai said quickly. 'I'm more than happy to take it in shifts. You can sleep in a bed and we won't have to disturb Riley and Darcy as they—'

'They'll be sleeping in a different room for tonight. I've already arranged everything with Martha and, besides...' He pointed to Hannah who was just climbing down from her booster seat to go and run after seven-year-old Ella and five-year-old little Martha. It was clear Hannah loved being around so many children. 'You have Hannah to worry about. Don't stress, Lore. Everything's going to be just fine,' he promised, but with the way she was starting to tremble with longing and hyperventilate with need each and every time he looked at her, she was beginning to wonder.

The next morning, Aidan was much improved.

'I still want him taken to Tumut hospital,' Woody told Aidan's parents. 'Even if it's just for one night. He needs to be monitored and also requires another course of IV antibiotics to guard against infection.'

'Does he really need to go? Can't you just give him more antibiotics here?' Martha asked, holding Aidan's hand tightly.

'Mum. It's OK,' Aidan tried to console her, a little embarrassed by his mother's fussing concern.

'He's right. We raised Aidan to be a fine young man.

He'll be fine, love,' Neil told his wife, giving her a little wink. Woody couldn't help but smile, pleased to see a happy couple. They reminded him of his own parents who, while they most certainly had their own ideals and ways of doing things, were still very happily married after almost forty years.

'Well, all right. If you and Lorelai think that's best,' Martha agreed, then looked around as though she only realised then that Lorelai was nowhere to be seen.

'She's still sleeping,' Woody supplied. 'She seemed so wiped out last night.'

Martha nodded. 'I know she was worried about how Hannah would sleep in a different place so perhaps she didn't get much sleep at all.' She looked from Aidan back to Woody. 'I'll go and check on her.'

'No. It's all right.' Woody could see quite clearly that Martha wanted to stay with her son for as long as she could. 'I'll go. You stay and fuss over Aidan some more. I know he secretly loves it.' With a grin he left the room, not at all certain he was up to seeing Lorelai this early in the morning. He'd almost been thankful to monitor Aidan throughout the night as if he'd been able to sleep, there was no doubt in his mind that his dreams would have been about Lorelai.

As he neared the lounge room where Lorelai and Hannah had been set up to sleep on the sofa bed, he heard the sound of sweet, soft giggles. He stopped just short of the doorway where he could quite clearly see the two Rainbow girls, lying on the sofa bed, Lorelai's arm around her daughter as they both looked up at the ceiling.

Lorelai pointed up. 'And look at that one, it looks just like a fluffy flower.'

Hannah giggled again and Woody closed his eyes

at the sound, loving the innocence of laughter but at the same time feeling such a piercing in his heart for everything he'd missed. His own daughter, Ja'tenya, would have been almost four years old, had she lived. His beautiful, precious baby.

'It's not a flower, Mummy,' he heard Hannah contradict. 'It's a squashed beetle.'

'Beetle?' Lorelai's laughter joined her daughter's and the sensations passing through Woody changed from one of past sorrow to present awareness. Gone were the remnants of his past, to be replaced by the vision of the lovely Lorelai. How was it possible that his heart could pound out such an erratic rhythm whenever he was close to her?

The previous evening, when he'd stood close to her, his body warmed through and through from her visual caress, he'd found it exceedingly difficult not to haul her into his arms and cover her sweet, plump lips with his own. It wasn't the first time he'd thought, pondered, dreamed of kissing Lorelai and he accepted now that it wasn't going to be the last.

'Woody!' Hannah's delighted squeals brought him back to the present and he quickly advanced further into the room. Lorelai sat up amongst the covers and ran her hands self-consciously through her hair whilst Hannah bounced around the bed on her knees, clapping her hands with delight. 'We just looking at the clouds,' Hannah pointed out matter-of-factly.

Woody frowned in confusion but smiled at the little girl. 'What do you mean?' He glanced at the ceiling above them which was painted a lovely creamy sort of colour, not a cloud in sight. 'I can't see any clouds.'

'No, silly. The 'tend clouds.' Hannah rolled her eyes

as though he were indeed quite thick. Woody instantly looked at Lorelai for some sort of translation.

'The clouds are pretend,' she said.

'See?' Hannah pointed to the ceiling. 'There's a monkey eating a banana. I like bananas.'

'Yes. Bananas are good,' he agreed.

'Some of the clouds we see are exceedingly specific,' Lorelai pointed out with a wide smile and stroked her hand lovingly over Hannah's hair.

'Have a look,' Hannah encouraged, and Woody came around the side of the sofa bed, kneeling down beside it before looking up at the ceiling to where Hannah pointed again. 'See? Now, that one is a elephant reading a book.'

'Oh, I see now,' he replied, and nodded. 'Good one. Oh, quick. Look over there.' He pointed to a different part of the ceiling. 'See? It's a jumping jelly-bean.'

Hannah giggled, then said quite seriously, 'I love jelly-beans.'

'Me, too,' Woody answered just as seriously, meeting Hannah's gaze. 'Did you have a good sleep, princess?'

Hannah nodded enthusiastically and looked at her mother, who seemed to be watching this exchange with quiet intent. 'I tuddled Mummy *all night*.' Hannah threw herself at her mother, Lorelai only just catching the child in time before receiving lots of quick pecking kisses from the three-year-old.

'Yes. We had a good sleep. How's Aidan? I'm presuming everything was all right last night otherwise you would have called me.'

'He's doing very well. I've already called Tumut hospital and they're sending an ambulance to come and collect him.'

'Great.' She was about to say more but Hannah obviously wasn't satisfied at the change in topic. She stood on the bed and held out her borrowed pink fairy nightie for Woody to inspect.

'Look at my fairy, Woody. She pretty.'

'She is. Just like you.' He winked, making Hannah giggle.

'And Mummy. Mummy's *weally* pretty, too.'

Woody turned to look at Lorelai, his gaze instantly turning serious. 'Yes. Yes, she is. Your mummy is *really* pretty, too.'

Lorelai met his gaze and found it impossible to look away. For a moment she didn't want to. She wanted to bask in the glory of a man who was openly expressing—albeit at the prompting of her daughter—that she was beautiful. It was something John had never done, not once in the entire time they'd been together. He'd never called her beautiful. He'd never just sat and stared, just looked at her, making her feel all warm and gooey inside, as Woody was doing now.

Her heart rate started to increase and her mouth went dry. She couldn't help it. Whenever Woody was around, her body would react with a powerful amount of awareness even though she'd spent a better part of the night lying awake, telling herself it was ridiculous for her to be flirting with the possibility of something romantic happening between herself and Woody. Even now, she longed for him to lean across, to close the distance between them and press his mouth to hers.

Woody nodded slowly. '*Really* pretty,' he echoed, as his gaze dipped to encompass her lips.

Hannah, distracted at hearing some of the other children playing down the hall, quickly scrambled from the bed and ran from the room, no doubt in search of a more appreciative audience. Within a split second the two adults found themselves alone...Lorelai sitting up amongst a mess of bedclothes whilst Woody knelt beside her, unable to look away.

'So...uh...why were you cloud-watching indoors?' His lips barely moved as he spoke but she watched the action closely, the way he formed the words, her sluggish mind taking a few seconds to process what he'd actually said.

'My mum had cancer. She was bedridden for quite some time and...uh...' Lorelai licked her lips and swallowed again, her throat dry, her heart still thumping out an erratic rhythm against her chest '...when I arrived home from school each day, I'd lie down next to her and even though she couldn't go outside, we'd...' She shrugged one shoulder.

'Cloud-watch,' they said in unison.

Woody nodded. 'That's a lovely story.'

Had he moved closer? He somehow seemed closer. She wasn't sure. When he was looking at her as though she were the most beautiful woman on the face of the earth, she wasn't sure of anything.

'Thanks.'

'Do you miss her?'

'Yes. I miss her. I miss Edward's parents. I miss everyone who's been taken from me, whether good or bad.' Her words were soft, barely a whisper, but she knew he'd heard.

In that one moment their hearts and minds connected and she found herself leaning closer towards him, no longer needing to speak words to convey what was on her mind. His eyes dipped to her mouth once again and she parted her lips, her breath fanning his cheek.

'Woody?'

He could hear the apprehension in her tone and he

wanted to reassure her, protect her, comfort her. For far too long, three long years, he'd wondered what it would be like to kiss her and right now he didn't care if a freak cyclone hit this very spot, nothing was going to stop him from following through on the urge that he could no longer deny.

'Shh.' He angled closer towards her until they were only a hairsbreadth apart. 'It's all right, Lore. This is meant to happen.'

'Meant to hap—?' She didn't even get to finish her sentence as Woody pressed his mouth firmly to her own.

CHAPTER SIX

LORELAI gasped, her eyelids fluttered closed, her breath slowly releasing the tension she'd been holding onto for far too long.

Woody was kissing her!

She'd dreamed of this moment and now it was happening. Actually happening. She didn't know what it meant. She had no rational thought to even figure it out and where that indecision, that inability to process would ordinarily scare her, right now she didn't want to think about anything other than wanting him closer, wanting his mouth on hers, wanting the sensations he was evoking deep within her to last for ever.

This was Woody. The man who had been such a rock to her during those initial hours after John's death. The man who had cared for and supported her throughout that first night, making her feel safe when she should have felt so vulnerable. Ever since then, whenever she'd felt at a loss, unable to cope with the emotions of what she'd lost, she would close her eyes and remember how protected she'd felt that night.

Since he'd arrived back in her life, her desire for him had only increased with each passing day. Her dreams were wild and vivid, the Technicolor moments infusing what she felt for him with what she so desperately wanted—for him to tell her he would stay in Oodnaminaby for ever.

Lorelai was looking for permanence, for a man she could share her life with, and at this moment in time she desperately wanted Woody to be that man. No other had ever made her feel so alive, so cherished, so respected. Surely, with such powerful sensations coursing between them, he had to realise that this attraction they felt towards each other was only the tip of the iceberg, the beginning of a whole new world?

He was in no apparent hurry to end the kiss, content to savour her sensations and flavours, committing them all to memory, and she basked in this knowledge, eager to move at the pace he set, almost desperate not to do anything wrong, lest he pull away. She wanted so much to please him, to make him want to kiss her again and again.

So perfect, so precious, so intoxicatingly pleasurable. It was as though their mouths were meant to be, fitting perfectly together, and as he leaned a little closer, wanting to slowly deepen the kiss, to share in the essence of this incredible woman, he knew that giving in to his weakness for her was going to cause him future pain.

But she'd been irresistible. Sitting in the messy bed, wearing a borrowed nightshirt, her blonde hair loose and tousled, making her look incredibly sexy. He was sure she'd had no idea just how beautiful she was, no idea what she did to him when she looked at him with those wide blue eyes of hers, or the way her tilting mouth made it impossible for him to resist kissing her.

He opened his lips a little wider and was more than pleased when Lorelai seemed to match his intensity, allowing him to lead her, to guide her through this storm of emotions that was creating havoc within both of them.

'Good morning,' he whispered against her lips, before indulging in a few more kisses.

He knew they should stop, knew he should pull back, put some distance between them, knew that the rest of the house would descend on them within a matter of minutes and that Lorelai might find it embarrassing to be caught kissing her colleague, but he couldn't help himself, needing just a few more quick kisses. Selfish, eager, desperate…addicted.

'I hear Hannah coming,' she murmured, pulling back and resting her forehead against his for a brief moment in an effort to control her breathing. She'd just leaned back against the pillows when Hannah came zooming around the corner and into the room, almost launching herself onto the bed. She was squealing with delight, quickly scrambling towards her mother, slipping between the rumpled bedclothes to hide from whoever was chasing her.

A moment later Steven, the second eldest, came into the room, pretending to growl like a monster. Hannah squealed and giggled and laughed, especially when a few more children came running in and followed her lead by slipping beneath the covers.

Lorelai looked at Woody, knowing the children were all too busy playing to even pick up on the undercurrents flowing between the two adults. There was no helping the embarrassment and uncomfortable sensations she was experiencing, especially when the children started tugging the covers from her. A moment later the covers slid from her legs. Little Martha was tugging at the sheet and Lorelai quickly pulled her nightshirt down as far as she could.

Woody smiled at the children's antics but Lorelai didn't miss the long, lingering look he gave her body. When he raised his gaze to meet hers, she could see, quite clearly, just how much he'd liked what he'd seen, his eyes glazed with a look of unveiled desire.

The realisation of such raw and unchecked emotion left her trembling.

'I'll go and see…' Woody pointed towards the doorway, trying to remember how to speak, but one glance at the incredibly sexy Lorelai and his words, as well as coherent thought, completely failed him. 'Er…someone.' With a nod, he quickly left the room, pushing both hands through his hair as though he was still trying to figure out what had just transpired between them.

Lorelai was everything he'd dreamed about—and more. Years ago, when he'd sat and watched her sleep through that long and painful night, he'd been attracted to her. Back then, he'd realised there was hope that one day he might be ready to move forward with his life, to leave the memory of his wife and daughter in the past.

Just now, having his mouth pressed against hers… had been heaven. She was an amazing woman and he could almost hear his sister's voice in his head telling him he'd chosen very well. Lorelai was a caring, thoughtful and giving woman and he should stop fighting the natural feelings he had for her. Perhaps it was time to move forward? To look towards some sort of future with Lorelai and Hannah?

His phone rang and he stopped in the hallway, absentmindedly extracting it from his trouser pocket. He was still pondering the way Lorelai's scent still floated around him, the way he could still feel the imprint of her mouth on his and the way he wanted nothing more than to do it again. He glanced at the caller ID, then froze.

Pacific Medical Aid.

He quickly pressed the button to ignore the call, his shoulders slumping a little as the reality of his world came crashing back over him. He wasn't free. For one brief second he'd forgotten his past, forgotten his commitment, forgotten the duty that would bind him for the rest of his life and had lived in the moment—the most glorious moment he'd had in far too long.

Woody closed his eyes. He shouldn't have kissed her. Kissing Lorelai only made things far more confusing than they already were. What had he been thinking? He hadn't. That was his main problem. He hadn't been thinking about his responsibilities. He hadn't been thinking about what he owed to Kalenia's family and their village in Tarparnii. He'd been selfish and he'd given in to the urge to press his mouth to Lorelai's.

He shook his head, completely unable to believe he'd actually followed through on his desire. The issue now was his difficulty in resisting the urge to head back in there, pull her into his arms and do it all over again.

Now he knew, now he understood, now he no longer needed to simply *dream* about kissing Lorelai because he'd experienced the *reality* of her luscious lips pressed against his. He'd discovered the answers to his questions about whether or not they'd be a compatible match. They were.

Surely now he had his answers he could move forward, put his infatuation with her behind him once and for all. He opened his eyes and exhaled harshly, rubbing his fingers to his temple, unable to believe his need for Lorelai appeared to have increased.

'Work.' The word propelled him into action and he

proceeded along the hallway to Aidan's room. He'd used work to get him through worse times than this, although he had to admit that even though it had been wrong, kissing Lorelai had felt so right. Her divine mouth, the sweet bouquet of her scent winding itself about him, hypnotising him, drawing him closer. She had the ability to make him forget everything. He couldn't let that happen.

Too much was at stake. Too many lives hung in the balance, depending on him. He couldn't afford to lose his focus. It wasn't worth it. His own wants and desires were superfluous to the greater picture, the greater responsibility of caring for his extended Tarparniian family.

It was up to him. They were counting on him and he wasn't going to let them down.

Lorelai was able to find time to snatch a quick shower and as she turned her face into the spray of the soothing hot water she closed her eyes, remembering another night, over three years ago…the last time she'd been sent off to have a shower whilst Woody was under the same roof.

After they'd left the accident site, the pain in Lorelai's heart had been like a lead balloon, exceedingly heavy. Woody had been her rock. He'd driven them home to Edward's house where Edward's younger brother, Hamilton, had been looking after Hannah. They'd collected the baby and when Lorelai had protested she didn't need Woody to see them home, saying that she'd be all right, Woody had flatly ignored her, saying he didn't want her to be left alone.

'Not tonight, Lorelai.' His words had been calm yet firm and his tone had brooked no argument.

When they'd arrived at her home, he'd ordered her to go and have a shower and freshen up whilst he changed Hannah's nappy. By that stage she'd been too numb to argue and had headed to the bathroom, eager to wash away the grime of her past and her grief for John. Beneath the spray she'd tried to cry, she'd tried to feel something—*anything*—but she'd been too numb.

When she'd emerged, she'd entered her bedroom to find Woody standing by the window, baby Hannah cradled in his arms, humming a lullaby. He'd had a lovely voice, deep and smooth, relaxing and hypnotic. She could understand why Hannah had fallen asleep. It was what she'd wanted. To lie down, to sleep, to find some peace, and she'd been incredibly grateful for Woody's foresight in offering to stay.

He'd seemed to sense her presence and turned to face her. 'Into bed,' he'd said, his tone brooking no argument. Lorelai had done as he'd suggested and once she had lain down, he'd placed the sleeping Hannah into her arms. She'd shifted onto her side, facing her daughter—the one good thing in her world.

Then Woody had placed his large, warm hand at the top of her spine where she'd held all her tension. Initially the touch had startled her, a mass of tingles spreading throughout her body, but after a split second he'd applied slight pressure with his fingers and rubbed in slow, small circles, the sensations instantly releasing Lorelai's stress. Her eyelids had closed and she'd sighed with relief as peace and calmness she'd thought she'd never feel again washed over her…and that was all she'd remembered, sleeping peacefully for quite some time.

She'd woken quite a few hours later, initially concerned as Hannah had no longer been in her arms. When she'd sat up, she'd seen Woody, resting in the chair beside the bed, Hannah snuggled into his arms, an empty baby's bottle on the bedside dresser. Man and babe had both been dozing and she'd watched them for a few minutes, intrigued at how someone so big and strong and masculine could look so incredibly sexy cradling her baby girl.

Lorelai had relaxed back into the mattress, turning her head on the pillow so she could continue watching man and babe, her eyelids slowing growing heavy once more. Woody had been there to help and support her. Just knowing he had been in the room, watching over herself and Hannah, had calmed her breathing and made the future she'd had to face less frightening…at least for the moment.

Then she'd woken up to find him gone. Even now, the memory of the way he'd left town without even saying goodbye still hurt. For some reason she'd always thought they'd formed a special connection that night, a bond of some sort, and until this morning she'd always thought she'd been wrong.

Sure, ever since Woody had arrived back in town she'd been drawn to him and, sure, there may have been a few occasions where she'd realised he might have felt that same tug but when he'd leaned forward and pressed his mouth against hers, everything had been confirmed.

Woody was attracted to her. Woody was interested in her. Woody hadn't been able to stop himself from following through on the urges both of them had been desperate to push aside.

As she turned off the taps and stepped from the shower, towelling herself dry, she couldn't help but wonder if there *had* been more to his leaving town so suddenly all those years ago. She didn't deny he'd been called back to Tarparnii but surely he hadn't had to disappear as easily as a magician?

Lorelai had thought she'd done something wrong, that she'd been too clingy that night or perhaps she'd said something to upset him. Try as she might, she couldn't recall anything that seemed out of place, especially during such a mind-numbing night.

She finished towelling herself dry and quickly dressed, hoping that now Woody had kissed her, now that they'd broken down that barrier, she had some hope of discovering why he'd left so suddenly that long ago morning.

They stayed with Aidan until the ambulance came and once the transfer was complete, Lorelai, Hannah and Woody said goodbye to Martha and Neil and their children before heading back to Oodnaminaby.

Throughout the past few hours Woody had been professional and polite, not once giving her a knowing look or an accidental touch or a secret smile. As Lorelai concentrated on driving, she sneaked a glance over at Woody, wondering if he'd say something now they were alone. Hannah was dozing in her car-seat, having expended a lot of energy running around with the other children that morning.

'At least Aidan will make a full recovery, thanks to you,' Lorelai said as the ambulance turned one way, heading towards Tumut, and they turned the other. The sun was out today, which often made it even more difficult for driving as a lot of the snow had melted beneath the hot rays. Lorelai concentrated, watching closely for black ice, but couldn't resist the extremely brief glance at the man beside her. Usually, he was talkative and yet, since he'd kissed her that morning, he'd hardly spoken a word to her except in a professional capacity, asking procedural questions about Aidan's transfer.

'I was just doing my job,' he replied.

'I know but still it's nice to be thanked.'

'True.' He continued to look straight ahead at the road and Lorelai wasn't sure what else to say. Ever since he'd left the room after the kiss, he'd been rather reserved. Was it because of the phone call he'd received? After he'd left the room, she'd quickly pulled on her jeans and had just stepped into the hallway when she'd heard his phone ring. Wanting to give him privacy, she'd been about to turn away but then he'd cancelled the call. After that she'd watched as his shoulders had sagged with dejection and she desperately wanted to know what was bothering him so much that a simple phone call could affect him in such a way.

Should she ask him about the call? She hadn't meant to pry, hadn't meant to be watching him, it had all just sort of…happened. Had the call been from PMA again? Had something gone wrong in Tarparnii? She shook her head, deciding the calls he received were none of her business, but at the same time she wanted him to know she was here to support him. She could sense something was wrong but try as she might to rack her brain for another topic to get them chatting, the only thing on her mind was why he'd seemed so aloof since their kiss.

The bottom line was she wanted to know. She needed to know how he felt and now seemed like the perfect time to ask him. 'Woody?' She cleared her throat, surprised to hear a slight hesitancy in her tone.

'Yes?'

Lorelai swallowed and forced herself to say the words that were currently swirling around and around in her mind, never seeming to find any sort of answers. 'Do you…regret what happened this morning?'

'This morning?' Woody gave a mild shrug. 'A lot of things happened this morning.'

'Woody!' Lorelai's exasperation escalated. 'Don't be dense. You know I'm talking about the kiss.'

'Oh. Right. Are you sure you want to discuss this now? While you're driving? The road looks quite dangerous and I'd hate us to have an acc—'

'We're not going to have an accident,' she said firmly. 'I've driven on these roads many times, in far worse conditions. I've engaged the all-wheel-drive and as it isn't even raining or snowing, it's not going to be that difficult to concentrate and talk, although given your present attitude and the way you appear to be avoiding the discussion, I'm guessing you just want to forget the kiss ever happened. Am I right?'

Woody closed his eyes for a brief moment, then shifted a fraction in his seat so he could look at her. 'It's not that simple, Lore.' His words were tinged with a hint of sadness and regret. Was that regret for the kiss or the fact that it wasn't simple?

'Sure it is. You either regret it or you don't, and just for the record I don't. Naturally, I was a little embarrassed after the actual, you know, event but that doesn't change the fact that I'm not sorry it happened. This was a big step for me to take, to give myself permission to move forward. As much as I really like you, Woody, and whilst I'm not at all ashamed of the beautiful kisses we shared, I've been trying to fight my attraction for you since you first arrived back in town.

'You have?'

She lifted her chin with that hint of defiance he'd seen on other occasions and he couldn't help but admire her. 'Yes. You're going to leave Ood again when your contract here is completed. Last time you upped and left without a word and although it was quite stupid of me at the time, I was hurt by your cool dismissal of me.'

'Lore, it wasn't like that.'

She held up a hand. 'Spare me. That was then, this is now. The point is that you'll be leaving and I'll be left trying to explain to Hannah why her beloved Woody has left her. Why he never comes over any more. She's attached herself to you and that's a bad thing. You are not a permanent fixture in her life and it's my job to protect her, as best I can, from emotional and physical hurts.'

'And that's why you didn't want to kiss me?'

'Yes…or at least that's why I've been trying to steer clear of you.' She gave him a quirky smile. 'I didn't succeed very well.' Lorelai sighed and they drove along for a few minutes in silence. 'At the moment I just want to know where I stand. You have quite a few more weeks here before Honey and Edward return and I think it's best if we set down some sort of rules or guidelines or… something.'

'Or something,' he mumbled.

'Look, during my marriage to John I was too scared to question him, to seek out the answers I so desperately wanted to know. I was weak and scared and I vowed to myself that if I ever found myself in a romantic situation again, I wouldn't be that way, I wouldn't allow myself to be the victim. If I wanted to know what was going on, I would ask…so I'm asking.'

'What do you want to know?'

'I want to know what the kiss meant to you. Did it mean *anything* to you? If you want to forget it, just say

the word and I'll forget it. We can go back to being simply professional colleagues for the remainder of your
time in town and then you can leave Ood and go and
do…whatever it is you do.'

She turned off the main road and headed towards
the Oodnaminaby medical clinic. She pulled the car
into the car park, Woody not saying a word. His silence
spoke volumes and she had a difficult time keeping her
tears under control and her heart from hammering right
through her chest.

'Right, then,' she remarked, her tone clipped, her
walls once more being erected to protect and preserve.
She needed to harden her heart, to keep herself and
Hannah safe. She kept the car engine running. 'I guess
your silence says it all. We'll forget the kiss ever happened. We'll ignore the attraction that sparks to life
every time we're within cooee of each other and we'll
simply be colleagues.' Hannah was starting to rouse in
the back seat and Lorelai was almost desperate to have
him out of her car.

'To that end, if you wouldn't mind doing the rest of
the patients this morning, Dr Moon-Pie, I'll go and get
Hannah organised. I'll do afternoon clinic so you can
go and sleep or shower or do whatever it is that you
want to do. It's certainly none of my business.'

'Lorelai—' he began.

'Out.'

'It's not that I don't want to—'

'Woody, I gave you the opportunity to say something. You didn't take it. Your silence said everything
and I'd appreciate it if you'd get out of my car. Now!'

He closed his mouth and nodded. It was better this
way…just so long as he didn't look at the pain and anguish he'd already glimpsed in her eyes. He opened the

door and stepped from the car, Lorelai reversing away from him almost before he'd properly shut the door.

He stood there and watched as she drove away, knowing he was doing the right thing but unable to believe how much it was hurting him.

For the next two weeks Lorelai was adamant in keeping her distance from Woody. She would nod politely to him if she bumped into him during clinic. She'd sit calmly and discuss patients with him and she'd answer any questions he had in an efficient and direct manner.

Aidan had been monitored in Tumut hospital, was recovering well from his impromptu surgery and was back helping his father around the farm during the mid-year school break. The snow season was now in full swing, with many families flocking from all around the country for their winter vacations. The clinics were busy with cuts, sprains and the occasional broken limb. Lorelai was more than happy for work to be hectic because it meant she could focus on her patients during the day and her exhaustion during the evenings.

Hannah, however, was starting to exhibit a little bit more attitude than usual and Lorelai wasn't sure why. 'Did you have a good day at Connie's?' she asked her daughter one evening as they walked towards their house, Hannah's purple and pink backpack in Lorelai's hand while her daughter stamped her way along the shovelled path, little puffs of steam coming from her mouth as she huffed.

'No. Tonnie got mad at me.'

Lorelai nodded, having already spoken to Connie about the incident, where Hannah had snatched a toy from one of the boys at the day-care centre, but she wanted Hannah to tell her about it.

'Why?' Her question was met with silence as they headed up their footpath. While Lorelai unlocked the door, Hannah picked up a handful of snow with her gloved hands and threw it at the garden gnome she'd decorated earlier that year as a Mother's Day present. The snowball hit the gnome fair in the face and Hannah nodded with satisfaction before heading inside, stamping the snow from her boots.

Inside, Lorelai bent down in the entryway and took off her gloves, helping an impatient Hannah to unbutton her coat. 'Hannah, what's really wrong, sweetheart? You can tell Mummy.'

Hannah angrily pulled off her gloves and beanie and threw them on the floor. Lorelai levelled her daughter a look that said she wasn't impressed with this behaviour. Hannah met her mother's gaze, held it for a fraction of a second as she tried to figure out just how far she could push her mother, then immediately bent and picked them up.

'What's made you so angry?' Lorelai asked, knowing something had been brewing for quite some time in the little girl's life. Hannah remained silent and Lorelai sighed, knowing she'd have to play twenty questions to drag the answer out of her. Hannah was as stubborn as her grandfather and some days Lorelai wanted to knock their heads together, hoping the stubbornness would fall out.

'Are you missing Aunty Honey and Uncle Edward? They sent you a postcard,' she said as she finished hanging their coats up in the drying cupboard before heading inside. Hannah followed but remained silent.

'Would you like me to ring Aunty Annabelle and ask her to bring the boys over so you can play with them?'

More silence, then a reluctant 'No'.

Lorelai shrugged as she sat down on the sofa and pulled Hannah onto her lap, the little girl instantly cuddling in. 'What's wrong, baby? Tell Mummy and I'll try to fix it.'

Hannah started crying and tears began to gather in Lorelai's eyes, wishing the little girl would tell her what was wrong.

'Wubduntlikeme,' Hannah mumbled, and Lorelai eased her back.

'What was that, sweetheart? I couldn't understand you.'

'Woody don't like me,' Hannah wailed, then really buried her face in her mother's neck and started to sob. At the mention of Woody, Lorelai tried not to stiffen.

'He...he...said we could read stories and he...he... don't do it, Mummy, and I *want* him to and Frankie said that Woody didn't like me.'

Lorelai rolled her eyes, realising that was the reason behind Hannah's bad behaviour that afternoon. 'Frankie is eight years old, Hannah, and eight-year-old boys often say things like that.'

'Woody don't like me,' Hannah wailed again as though she didn't really understand what the words meant but knew they weren't good.

'Of course Woody likes you,' Lorelai instantly soothed. 'Of course he does.' She held her little girl close and kissed her head.

'But he don't come over and read the stories to me.'

'He's been very busy at work, sweetheart,' Lorelai tried to explain, but when she looked into Hannah's eyes, seeing the utter misery in the blue depths, she knew there was only one thing to do. Like any loving parent, she was willing to sacrifice her own emotions in favour of her child. If she was honest with herself, she'd admit her own behaviour, desperately wanting Woody close but knowing she needed to keep him at a distance, didn't make any sense to her heart. The man was enigmatic and she wondered whether she'd ever understand him.

However, now, even though she knew Hannah's reaction was merely a taste of what was to come when Woody eventually left town, as he was still in the area and she could do something to fix Hannah's distress, perhaps she could bend the rules, just this once, and see if Woody was available to pop by for a visit. Purely for Hannah, she told herself quickly, but all the while knowing she was lying. She simply didn't seem capable of self-control where Woody was concerned and neither, it seemed, was Hannah.

'I have a suggestion,' she said, forcing a smile into her words. 'Why don't we call him on the phone right now and ask him to come over and have some soup with us? Then, after you've eaten all your soup, you and Woody can sit and read before bedtime. Does that sound like a good idea?'

Hannah lifted her head and stared at her mother, hope lighting her little face. Then, as though by magic, the tears vanished and little blue eyes blinked brightly at her. 'Weally? I can speak to him on the phone?'

'Sure can.'

With a single bound Hannah was off Lorelai's lap and heading towards the phone, quickly bringing the cordless handset back to her mother. 'Call him now, Mummy. Call him *now*!'

'OK. Just…' Lorelai patted the sofa cushion next to her, trying to squash down her own nervousness. She'd been intent on keeping her distance from Woody, knowing it was better this way, to simply be colleagues with him rather than to give in to the memories of the powerful kiss they'd shared.

She'd worked hard to control her dreams, thankful the exhaustion from busy days helped her to sleep at night, but every morning, without fail, he was her first thought whenever she opened her eyes. In her dreams, he'd visited her, he'd held her, he'd kissed her more passionately, more intimately than he had before. He'd looked down into her face, caressing her cheeks, her lips, her neck with his soft fingers before covering the same path with small intoxicating butterfly kisses, turning her insides to mush and making her knees buckle.

The phone was ringing and Lorelai braced herself.

'Hello?' His deep, rich voice came down the line and her eyelids instantly fluttered closed, her heart beating even more rapidly than it had when his lips had been on hers.

She opened her mouth to say something but found the words stuck in her throat, her mouth as dry and as scratchy as sandpaper.

'Hello?' he said again, and she could hear the confusion in his tone. 'Crank calls in Oodnaminaby. Something I hadn't quite expected,' he continued.

'Mummy? Is he dere?' Hannah asked, her words earnest.

Woody must have heard her in the background because the next words out of his mouth were, 'Lore? Is that you?' His tone had gentled somewhat and Lorelai closed her eyes, allowing the sensation to wash over her for a split second before pulling herself together. Opening her eyes and clearing her throat, she nodded, even though he couldn't see her. 'What's wrong? Is something wrong?' he asked before she could get a word out. She could hear him moving around and a second later there was the sound of a door closing.

'No. Everything's fine,' she finally managed to grind out, forcing herself to swallow and her heart rate to settle. She had to breathe, to get herself under control. 'It's, uh…Hannah. She wants to talk to you.'

'Oh. Great. I've really missed her.' And he sounded as though he really meant it. Lorelai quickly gave the phone to her daughter, who took the receiver with both hands and brought it to her face so she could talk to him.

'Woody?'

'Hey, there, princess,' Lorelai heard him say. She shook her head and stood up, heading into the kitchen to put the kettle on. She needed a soothing cup of herbal tea, something to calm her nerves, to stop her world from spinning simply because she'd heard the caring urgency in Woody's voice when he'd assumed something was wrong.

She walked back towards Hannah, checking on her daughter and couldn't help the smile that touched her lips at the sight of the three-year-old lying back on the cushions, holding the receiver with one hand while she twirled her hair with the other, giggling into the phone. 'A glimpse of the future,' she murmured, and pleased her daughter was happy once more returned to the kitchen to make her tea and warm up the soup they were having for dinner.

No sooner had she placed the dish into the microwave than the doorbell rang. Frowning, she wiped her hands on a tea-towel and headed for the door, Hannah running ahead of her.

'He here. He here,' she said, the phone receiver still to her ear.

'Who's he—?' Lorelai didn't even get a chance to

finish her sentence as she realised that Woody had been walking to her house whilst talking to Hannah on the phone. Who else would Hannah be referring to? No one!

'Hurry, Mummy.' Hannah demanded, jumping around beside the entryway door, excitement bursting from every part of her little body.

'All right. Just shift out the way and let me through.' Lorelai waited for her daughter to move, then opened the door. There they stood, staring over the threshold at each other, her heart instantly skipping a beat from one of his half-smiles aimed in her direction.

'Hi.' The word was soft yet deep and lovely and gorgeous, warming her through and through. He was dressed in his warm coat and scarf. He wore no gloves but still had his phone to his ear. He shifted his gaze to encompass Hannah. 'Hello, Miss Hannah.' His smile was a wide, beaming one that caused Lorelai to put a hand to the wall in order to steady herself.

'Woody!' Hannah thrust the phone receiver at her mother before launching herself at him. He bent down and scooped her up, slipping his own phone into his coat pocket. Lorelai simply stood behind the door as he entered, carrying her daughter in his arms, leaving her feeling very much like the third wheel.

CHAPTER SEVEN

AFTER dinner, and with Woody helping Hannah to finish up that last bit of soup in her bowl, the little girl
began insisting it was time for her beloved Woody to
read her some stories.

From the moment he'd walked through Lorelai's front
door, Woody had been his usual self. Charming, funny
and relaxed. The change in him from the man she'd been
doing her best to avoid at the clinic was acute and she
had to admit she enjoyed this version of him far more
than the polite, professional one.

This was *her* Woody, the man she couldn't stop
thinking about. It was all highly confusing and at times
she found herself on edge, watching him closely, trying
to decipher if there were hidden messages in his words
and actions but she could find none.

She was almost desperate to relax in his presence, to
find joy in his company as she had right up until that
morning when they'd kissed. She'd glanced at him several times across the table, unable to believe the way
one simple smile from him had had the ability to turn
her body to mush. Did the man have any idea of the
hold he had over her?

Lorelai still couldn't understand why he'd withdrawn
from her after that incredible kiss. Never before had

something so simple, such as Woody's mouth against her own, rocked her world in such a way. Being with Woody, being in his arms, being so close to him, had felt so right. She still struggled with the pain and devastation at his rejection, confused about why he didn't feel the same way.

Even in those few moments afterwards, when she'd rested her head against his, the two of them breathing heavily, she'd felt a connection pass between them. She'd thought he'd felt it too. It was as though in that one moment time had stopped and their hearts had bonded. The odd sensation hadn't left her since but obviously she'd been wrong and Woody hadn't felt the connection after all.

'He was playing with you,' she'd told her reflection just that morning. Where she'd thought he wasn't like John, that he didn't need to have every woman he met fall in love with him, she was starting to think she'd been wrong. He certainly enjoyed the attention of women, continuing to be his charming, charismatic and chivalrous self towards every one he met. Even the men in town thought he was the 'bees knees', as one of her older patients had termed it.

However, she'd also noticed that his smile didn't hold as long, that the light didn't reach his eyes. He still provided excellent care to all their patients but something was missing and it had taken her a while to realise it was his natural spark. Somehow it had dimmed.

The nurturer within her had wanted to talk to him about it, to help him out, to offer to be a friend, to listen and support, but she knew that even if she'd offered, he'd have turned her down. He'd made his position clear on the drive back from Martha's farm when he'd remained quiet, withdrawing from her presence.

Tonight, however, he was as relaxed and at ease as the first time she'd met him. He paid close attention to Hannah and as she watched them interact, Lorelai was struck by a different train of thought. Perhaps the reason why he'd pulled back after their kiss had been because he'd thought he was being unfaithful to the memory of his wife.

Was that it? Was that why he'd withdrawn from her? When she'd been unable to stop staring at him while he'd stretched his limbs, he'd told her the last woman to look at him in such a way had been his wife. Was that a good thing?

She had to remember that *her* marriage hadn't been a happy one. Therefore, she was eager to move forward, to have new and exciting experiences. For Woody, moving forward might be more difficult. Her heart welled with concern for him and she shook her head, as though to clear her thoughts.

'Something wrong?' Woody asked, and she belatedly realised he'd been watching her. She met his gaze, desperate to ignore the way her heart hammered its momentarily uneven rhythm whenever his deep blue eyes stared at hers in such a fashion. She could hear the honest concern in his tone, could see it in his eyes, and it only succeeded in confusing her even more. He cared about her. That much was clear. He cared about Hannah, too, otherwise he wouldn't have bothered to come tonight. So if he cared about both of them, why was he erecting walls to keep them both at a distance?

'I'm fine.' Lorelai turned her attention to Hannah, who was carefully climbing down from her booster seat.

'Storwee time, storwee time,' she kept saying over and over, excitement in her tone.

'Go and get changed for bed first,' Lorelai instructed as Woody helped her carry the dirty dishes to the sink.

'But, Mummy! It's storwee time!' Hannah looked at her mother as though Lorelai was cuckoo.

'Yes, and story time is usually when you lie down in your bed and we read a book together. Do you need help getting out of your clothes?' She held her hands out towards her headstrong three-year-old.

Hannah stamped her foot and crossed her arms over her chest, clearly displeased with the scheduled programme of events. 'It's storwee time!'

'I'd watch your attitude, young lady,' Lorelai stated clearly, not breaking eye contact with her impertinent daughter. 'It would be a shame for Woody to have to leave early and without reading you one single story simply because you couldn't control your temper.'

Hannah's eyebrows rose at that and she quickly backed down. Woody couldn't help but admire Lorelai's way of handling her daughter, firm but fair. He put down on the bench the dishes he was carrying, then crouched down beside Hannah.

'I have an idea. Why don't you go and choose three stories for us to read? You bring them here to me and then while you're getting ready for bed and brushing your teeth, I'll get the kitchen all sorted out for Mummy. Then we can sit down and read stories. How about that?'

Hannah thought for a moment, tilting her head to the side, a very serious look on her face, and Lorelai quickly turned away, unable to keep a straight face due to the gorgeous posture of her thoughtful daughter. So adult. She glanced at Woody and saw he was having an equally difficult time to keep from chuckling at the three-year-old.

'Hmm… Otay.' With that, she ran off to her room

in search of the story books. Woody stood and turned to face Lorelai.

'She's really becoming a handful, isn't she?' he asked rhetorically as he started rolling up his sleeves.

'She's three. No one ever tells you that the terrible twos start when they're about eighteen months old and the four-year-old's temper tantrums start when they're three.' She shrugged and sighed. 'There's not a day goes by that we don't have a disagreement about something. Peter and Annabelle keep telling me it's normal. Out of all of Edward's brothers, they're the only ones who have children. I would have been so lost without their help and support, even if it's just to hear the words "It's normal" or "She'll grow out of it".' She tried to laugh but it ended up coming out as a sigh.

Woody gave her a small, heartfelt smile. He wanted to put his hand on her shoulder, to reassure her, to encourage her, but he knew any physical contact with Lorelai would only result in him losing his self-control once again. 'Well, either way, you're doing a great job. You held firm, you didn't give in, and one day Hannah will respect you for letting your yes be yes and your no be no.'

'You sound as though you've had a lot of practice with children and yet you're not even an uncle yet. Honey's not due to have the baby for another few months.'

'I was raised in what some people would call a hippy commune, several different communes, in fact.'

'Oh, that's right. I forgot about that. Honey always said there were a lot of other children around.'

'Always, and a lot of the time, our parents were away protesting one thing or another.'

Lorelai moved around the kitchen, filling the kettle

and switching it on, doing her best to avoid accidentally touching Woody. He began rinsing the dirty dishes.

'You don't have to do that,' she interjected. 'I can do them later.'

'It's fine, Lore. I'm more than used to pitching in. As you've just pointed out. I was raised in a commune where everyone pitched in with everything. Cooking, cleaning, dishes.'

'Even the children?'

'Especially the children. We did move around a lot. A new place every now and again depending on where my parents were protesting next. Honey and I went to a lot of different schools, as did all the other children in communes. Generally we stuck together, both at home and in the schoolyard.'

Lorelai smiled as she pulled two cups from the cupboard. She held one up towards him, silently asking him if he wanted tea. Woody nodded in agreement. 'Did you ever get into any fights?'

He looked at her and raised an eyebrow of surprise. 'With a surname like Moon-Pie? You are joking, right? Honey and I were teased at every school and, yes, I did have quite a few after-school fights but...' he held up his finger as though needing to making his point clear '...it was always in defence of others. Honey used to give me an earful whenever she cleaned up my scratches and grazes. She was quite the little doctor back then.' He shook his head as though bemused by the memory.

'And your parents? What did they say?'

'Nothing much. We'd been raised to fight for our rights, not necessarily with physical violence, but my dad was proud of me for defending my sister and the other kids in the commune.'

'Such a different way of life. Honey practically rais-

ing you and the other children in the commune and there
you were, defending people's honour and making sure
no one was picked on.'

Woody nodded as he finished rinsing the dinner
dishes. 'It may have seemed strange to outsiders but
it was a good life, even though it was probably more
higgledy-piggledy than others.'

Lorelai smiled at his turn of phrase, then heard a
light grunting coming from the direction of the hallway. She turned to find Hannah walking back into the
room, almost crushed beneath the weight of three very
large story books. Lorelai laughed as she took them off
Hannah. 'Woody said *three* stories. Not three *volumes*.'

Relieved of her precious books and pausing only
to draw in a rejuvenating breath, Hannah reached for
Lorelai's hand. 'Tum on, Mummy. Hurry!'

Lorelai didn't want to go with her daughter, instead
wanting to stay with Woody, to ask him more questions.
He'd been quite open with her, talking to her as they had
before the kiss. Perhaps there was some hope that even
though he'd backed off on the romantic front, they'd be
able to salvage some sort of friendship. Their worlds
were going to be loosely linked anyway as Woody's
sister was her best friend.

As she finished dressing Hannah in her nightie,
slippers and dressing gown, she couldn't help but
worry about her daughter's attachment to Woody. As
soon as Honey and Edward returned, he would leave
Oodnaminaby and go—wherever it was he was off to
next. Hannah wouldn't have the luxury of simply calling him up on the phone and asking him to come over
to read her stories and Lorelai wasn't quite sure how
she was going to explain Woody's prolonged absence.

'Hurry, Mummy,' Hannah said as Lorelai tried to brush the little white teeth. 'Woody's waiting for me.'

'Then stop talking,' Lorelai grumbled, almost jealous of the fact that Hannah was right. Woody *was* waiting for her, more than content to give her daughter all the attention she deserved. So why couldn't he give *her* the same attention? Why had he backed off from the kiss?

As Hannah spat out the toothpaste and rinsed her mouth, before running from the room to no doubt launch herself at Woody, Lorelai realised that in order to silence the questions rolling around in her mind, she needed to find answers.

Perhaps when Hannah was in bed asleep, she'd be able to talk to him, to ask him once more what had happened. Why he'd gone from being so hot and sexy and flirty towards her to being ice-cold and withdrawn? If it was something to do with his wife, perhaps she could help him through it, help him to move forward. Maybe if she understood where he was coming from, she'd be able to let go of her own attraction towards him and move forward with *her* own life, treating Woody as nothing more than a family friend.

She tidied up and prepared Hannah's bed, hoping her daughter would fall asleep in Woody's arms while he read to her. At least that way Lorelai could avoid a tantrum about Hannah not being sleepy and not needing to go to bed.

When she eventually headed out, she found her kitchen to be spotless and a cup of tea waiting for her on the bench. She couldn't help the swell of appreciation at what he'd done for her. Something so small as making her a cup of tea, of tidying her kitchen—it was wonderful. As she collected her cup and walked into the lounge room, finding Hannah sitting on Woody's lap, completely engrossed in a story, it made her realise just how lonely her life had become.

Of course she had her father, who usually came around for dinner at least once a week, and she had Honey and Edward, as well as Peter and Annabelle and their children, plus countless of friends in Ood whom she loved dearly, but it wasn't the same as coming home to someone, sharing her thoughts, her hopes and dreams with someone special—someone like Woody.

She slid into the big armchair and watched him hold her daughter as though she were the most precious little thing in the world. It was the classic picture of domestic bliss, something she had hoped to find with John, but those dreams had been crushed.

Now her bundle of love, the apple of her eye for the past three and a quarter years, was starting to yawn, her eyelids beginning to become heavy as Woody continued reading to her, the brightly coloured hard-bound story book open before them.

Lorelai sipped her tea again and sighed into the chair, allowing his deep, relaxing tone to wash over her. Woody was so different from John. He was dependable, honest and hard-working. He was reliable and thoughtful. The way he was with Hannah, the way he gave her all his attention, was wonderful. As Hannah slumped further into Woody's arms, her eyes now closed, her breathing starting to even out into a deeper rhythm, Lorelai was overwhelmed with a sense of peace.

It was very rare she ever felt so at ease, so relaxed, as though it didn't matter what had happened in the past or what might happen in the future. Right here, right now, she was quite content. The last time she'd felt this way had been after John's accident when, distraught and confused, Woody had brought her home from the accident site. She didn't know what it was about him but whenever he was near, she couldn't help the sense of...completeness which seemed to surround her.

'"And then the prince looked down into the eyes of his beautiful princess and knew they would live happily ever after,"' Woody read, his tone soft and clear. 'Is Princess Hannah asleep, now, Lore?' he continued in the same voice, and Lorelai smiled.

'She is.'

Woody closed the book and placed it beside him before carefully shifting Hannah more comfortably into the cradle of his arms, the three-year-old moaning a little before settling into him, more than content.

'I'll just sit here a while to make sure she's really asleep,' he said softly. 'The last thing we want is for her to wake up the instant we put her into bed.'

Lorelai nodded. 'Thank you, Woody. You have such a deep, relaxing voice, I thought I was going to drop off as well.'

He shrugged one shoulder, images of a sleeping Lorelai flashing quickly into his mind. The last time he'd watched her sleep, he'd had a difficult time keeping himself under control. She'd looked so peaceful, so serene, so incredibly lovely. He'd felt her pain, her loss and he'd done his best to stand by her side, to protect her through the night. Whatever she had needed, he had been there on hand to help. When Hannah had started to awaken, he'd quickly removed the babe from her mother's arms, changed her, prepared a bottle for her and cuddled her back to sleep. The same beautiful little girl he was now cradling in his arms as she snuggled into him, sleeping peacefully once more. That night he'd felt a connection not only to Hannah but to Lorelai as well. She'd had a whole new life ahead of her and there was no way he could have been a part of it back then, just as he couldn't be a part of her life now. He had too many responsibilities.

'Feel free to drop off into slumberland, Lore. I'll cope with tucking Hannah into bed and seeing myself out.'

'Would you tuck me into bed, too?' The words were out of her mouth before she could stop them.

'Uh…Lore…um…' Woody's eyes widened at her question and he couldn't believe how he found himself so tongue-tied, such was the power she held over him. The more time he spent with her, the more he came to know her. And the more he came to know her, the more his feelings grew. 'I would definitely make sure you were comfortable enough to sleep through the night and ensure you didn't wake up with a crick in your neck,' he replied, after clearing his throat a few times.

Lorelai smiled. 'You're a good man, Woody, and, believe me, they're hard to find.' She put her cup down on the small table beside her chair and stretched her arms above her head, watching beneath hooded lashes as Woody seemed to follow her body's actions with great interest. His careful caress warmed her, giving her a touch of confidence.

'Woody? Why have you been…um…distant from me? The real reason, please? I think you owe me at least that much.'

'Oh, Lore.' He closed his eyes for a moment and exhaled slowly before looking at her. 'My life is incredibly complicated and, despite how being with you makes me feel, I can't change it.'

Lorelai processed his words for a moment. 'How is it complicated? I'm presuming it has something to do with the death of your wife but surely I can help you in some way to deal with the pain of loss.' She angled her head to the side, a small sad smile touching her lips. 'I've unfortunately become quite an expert on dealing with the loss of loved ones.' She leaned forward in her chair, her hands clasped together, her words earnest.

'Please let me help you. Please allow me to be there for you, to listen to you, to support you. Becoming lost in grief can end up being a lonely road if you don't have caring people to tether yourself to. We can put on a brave face, we can nod and smile and make decisions. We can walk through our lives for years, the pain being shut away in some dusty corner of our mind, only to burst forth when we least expect it, unleashing the agony that's been festering and lurking there.'

Lorelai nodded slowly. 'I *do* know how you feel, Woody. How empty the loss can leave you, but not dealing with it isn't healthy.' She looked down at her hands. 'I know you have Honey, your parents and grandparents. I know you have countless friends you can rely on, and if you have someone who's helping you with this, then by all means tell me to back off and mind my own business, but...' She stopped again and sighed. 'I can see the emptiness you've tried so hard to hide for so long. I can only see it because I've felt it.'

Woody was silent for a moment, her words hanging in the air. He looked down at Hannah, now completely out to the world, off hopefully having lovely dreams of princes and princesses who always found their happily ever after, no matter who or what tried to prevent them. He had loved deeply and he had lost deeply. Now, being here with Lorelai, he was doing his best to ignore the way she made him feel, the way Hannah's innocence surrounded his heart, making him think about the child he'd lost, the child who would have by now been a little older than Hannah. So much pain. So much loss, a loss he'd never thought he'd be able to deal with, a loss that still bound him with responsibilities of honour and support.

He lifted his eyes to meet Lorelai's, the artificial glow of the lamps casting a halo around her, making him wonder if she wasn't some sort of angel sent from above to help him to let go of his past anguish and move forward into the light, into the land of the living.

'Who helped *you*?' His words were soft but he wanted to know. Lorelai was surrounded with people who loved her, who cared about her, who would always be there to support her, so who was the person she'd anchored herself to in order to deal with her husband's death.

'Who helped me? *You* did.'

CHAPTER EIGHT

'*ME?*'

Her words had astounded him.

'Yes. You were right beside me when I learned John was dead.'

'But…' He shifted in the chair, Hannah murmuring something inaudible as he moved. 'Oh.' Woody looked down at the sleeping child as though he'd momentarily forgotten she was there. 'Let me put Hannah into her bed,' he said, needing just a few minutes to process Lorelai's revelation.

Woody stood and carried Hannah to her room, tenderly laying the child on her waiting bed. Lorelai pulled up the covers and bent to kiss her daughter. 'Sleep sweet, princess,' she murmured, before the two of them headed back to the living room.

Woody stood, not wanting to sit, needing to move around in order to figure out just *how* he'd been able to help Lorelai. He shoved his hands into the pockets of his denim jeans as Lorelai went and fiddled with the heating controls.

'Lore,' he began when it appeared she wasn't going to elaborate. 'Please explain how I could possibly have been the person to help you through your grief? I left the day after the accident and I didn't see you for over three years. How could I have helped you?'

Lorelai sighed and smiled, a sense of calm washing over her. Woody appeared ready to talk, to finally open up to her, and she knew this was the next step in their burgeoning relationship.

'Hannah was born right here—in this room. Your sister delivered her.' Lorelai pointed to where Hannah's birth had taken place. 'John had told me earlier that night that he was leaving me, that I was useless as a wife and that he didn't want either me or the baby. If it hadn't been for Honey and Edward, and especially Hannah, I wouldn't have made it through that first fortnight.'

She tidied up the story books as she talked then turned to face him. 'Do you remember the first time we met? You'd just come to town and we had a big family dinner to meet you.' Lorelai smiled. 'You were tall and handsome and exuded joviality. We were quite a party for dinner that night, all of us filling Hannah's and Cameron's big house with rowdy laughter again.'

Woody nodded. 'It was a good night.'

'It was and through all the smiles and happiness and laughter, when you thought no one was looking, the smile would slip and your eyes would reflect such pain. The pain of loss. I only recognised it because after watching my mother die and then losing Edward's parents, it was something I'd learned to detect. Of course, I felt uncomfortable asking you about it because we'd only just met and, besides, I was largely preoccupied with a newborn and a heart filled with pain.'

'Yet you soldiered on.' He smiled. 'You're a strong woman, Lorelai. I've always admired that about you and you've done a wonderful job of raising Hannah.'

'I've had great support.'

'Then how can you say *I* was the one to help you through your grief over John?'

'Because you made me feel secure. You made me feel protected. You made me feel as though I was still worthy as a person. When John rejected me, he destroyed more than our marriage. He destroyed my self-esteem.' Her voice cracked a little on the words and Woody's need to protect her kicked into overdrive.

'Before we met, Honey had told me what that oaf had done to you, what he'd said and how he'd treated you.' Woody clenched his hands into fists. 'I was as angry as the rest of the Goldmark clan, even though I'd never met the man. When we first met, I had just become a card-carrying member of the "protect Lorelai" brigade.'

She chuckled softly at his words. 'That was Peter's idea and it was a sweet gesture. It made me feel so loved by my family. But I noticed one other thing that night, something that astounded me.'

'What's that?'

'I found you very attractive.' She felt incredibly self-conscious in confessing such a thing and after looking into his surprised eyes she realised he might take her words the wrong way. 'Not that it was astounding I found you attractive,' she quickly clarified. 'Merely the fact that after everything that had happened to me, I was still able to *feel* that way again.'

'I understood your meaning and I'm…speechless.' He paused, unable to believe how warmed he felt at her words. 'Back then? Really? You were attracted to me?'

Lorelai nodded. 'My husband had left about a fortnight before, I'd given birth to a baby and yet, when I looked at you, I felt…feminine.' She shook her head and frowned, a small, shy smile on her lips. 'I can't explain it properly but feeling those emotions let me see there was more to life than what was presently taking place within my little world. It showed me the damage John had done wasn't permanent and that in time I would be able to move on, to one day open my heart again and love someone new.

'Then John died…' She trailed off, closing her eyes for a moment. 'I can still see him, trapped in that car. I can still hear you urging me to go home, but I couldn't.' She paused to control the emotion in her voice. 'That night, I'd just stood there, unable to move while you helped John. I was desperately waiting for someone else to come so that *you* could take me home—my knight in shining armour.'

Woody frowned. 'Armour? I'm no hero, Lore.'

'You were for me. I needed you that night and you stepped up to the plate, you helped me, supported me, cared for me. I didn't want to go home alone and you knew that. You refused to take no for an answer and you stayed with Hannah and me. You showed me compassion, you kept me safe, you gave me rest.'

Lorelai licked her dry lips and opened her eyes to look up at him. 'You brought us back here and all I really remember is you giving my neck and shoulders a rub as I lay on my bed, cuddling my baby girl, tears unable to fall.' She stepped forward, closing the distance between them, and reached out to touch her fingers to his cheek. He didn't flinch, didn't pull away, didn't move. Instead, he simply looked into her upturned face, a look of incredulity in his gaze at what she was saying.

'I also remember waking up and seeing you sleeping in the chair, Hannah in your arms. You cradled her as though she were the most precious little girl in the world.' She went to drop her hand back to her side but

Woody quickly reached for it, lacing his fingers with hers. At the touch, she gasped. Her mind faltered, as it always did with one sweet touch from Woody.

'Your actions and your support gave me hope, even if it only was for a short time. I don't understand why you left so suddenly. For years I've kept thinking I must have done something wrong to drive you away, even though Honey assured me you left because you were needed in Tarparnii.'

Woody swallowed and Lorelai's gaze dipped to his lips, the warm atmosphere surrounding them becoming fraught with longing as he still desperately tried to fight his natural and instinctive reaction to this woman.

'You didn't do anything wrong, Lore.' He shook his head. 'It was all me. I was the one who had done something wrong.'

'But…how? Woody, I don't understand.'

'Lore, the reason I left that morning, why I hightailed it out of Oodnaminaby, was purely and simply because the emotions I felt towards you were…overwhelming.'

She blinked slowly as his words filtered through her mind. 'What!' It had been the last thing she'd expected him to say.

'From the moment we met, Lorelai, things haven't run smoothly. I can't explain it. I don't even understand it but at that first dinner, I was…aware of you, too. Ridiculous. Stupid.' He shrugged. 'Unexplainable. I'd come to town to see Honey, to spend time with my sister and check out this man she was obviously in love with, and instead I found myself interested in you…*drawn* to you. I was stunned at my reaction, not because you're not worthy of it,' he quickly clarified with a smile, 'but more because no other woman had ever drawn me in like that, except for my wife.' Woody paused for a moment, letting the words settle over them. 'The guilt swamped me. Guilt for remaining alive. Guilt for moving on with my life which, in turn, brings with it the guilt I've been carrying around for four years, ever since the death of my family.'

'Family?' Her eyes widened in shock. 'You had children?'

'One baby. A daughter.'

'Oh, Woody,' she breathed, empathy in her tone. 'What pain you must have suffered.'

Lorelai gave his hand a little squeeze, wanting to encourage him, wanting him to know she was there, she was happy to listen, to return the favour and support him in his time of need. She didn't rush him and waited patiently for him to continue.

'Kalenia and I met when I was in Tarparnii for my third stint with PMA only this time I wasn't there as a medical student but as a qualified surgeon. I was fresh out of medical school, this boy genius who was more of a novelty in Australia than anything else.'

'A novelty?'

'Honey never told you? I started medical school when I was seventeen and completed it in four years.'

'Four years?' Lorelai blinked one long blink. 'I mean, Honey's always called you a genius but I always thought that was more of a big-sister "I'm proud of you" type of thing. Wow. Four years! I take it you went into surgery after that?' While she spoke, Woody led them both to the sofa but made no effort to remove his hand from hers as they sat down.

'I did. They made an exception for me and again I completed the training quite quickly. By the age of twenty-four I was over working in Tarparnii. Honestly,

Lore, that country is so beautiful. I'd love to show it to you one day.'

'I'd love to see it,' she replied, secretly delighted at the way he'd spoken of a future together.

'Kalenia spoke beautiful English and was often used by PMA as a translator. She travelled to a lot of very unsafe places with our teams as we worked to provide effective medical care. We fell in love and were married in the traditional Tarparnese festival, the *par'Mach,* which is a sort of big wedding. Kalenia became pregnant almost straight away but when she was only seven months gone, she gave birth to our daughter, Ja'tenya.'

'Oh, Woody. Was she…?'

'A fighter? She was. She may have been at a disadvantage but she was a fighter, my girl. Being in the jungle, it's difficult to look after neonate babies, but at that time Honey had come across for a visit and was able to bring her expertise to help me deal with what was going on. Ja'tenya started to put on weight. She started to feed more regularly and with increasing ease. She started to make little gurgling noises, to smile.'

A light touched his eyes, his face lighting with love as he spoke of his daughter, of the happiness she'd brought him. Then, just as quickly as it had come, the light began to fade and the smile disappeared from his lips.

'Then *Yellom Cigru* fever spread through the village. It's a Tarparniian disease that acts like bad flu and unfortunately most babies are susceptible to it, especially neonates.' He rubbed his free hand over his face, then looked at her. 'Telling Kalenia that our eight-week-old baby girl had died was possibly the worst moment of my life.'

Lorelai couldn't believe the pain she felt, the way

his anguish had somehow become her own. 'How did Kalenia take the news?'

'Badly. She'd already stopped coming out with our team as a translator when she'd become pregnant but she'd always been very active in her village. Not now. She didn't come out of our hut for well over a month. Then, one week, when I was off with a team doing a clinic in a village over a day's drive from where we lived, I received word that a carrier with the *clollifon* disease had been staying in the village.'

'What's that?'

'*Clollifon* is a Tarparniian disease that attacks the immune system of the natives. Usually if it's caught early enough a good course of antibiotics can kill it but if a person's already been ill, with flu-like symptoms, the outcome is far worse. There had been several outbreaks on the other side of the country but...' He stopped and collected his thoughts. 'Kalenia hadn't been eating properly since Ja'tenya's death and quickly contracted the disease.'

Woody closed his eyes and shook his head. 'By the time I returned to the village, she had hours left to live. Her father had been treating her, giving her natural remedies and a few of the Western medicines that were stored in the village, but none had worked.' When he opened his eyes, there were no filters on his soul and Lorelai could see quite clearly the anguish he'd lived through.

'Things didn't improve after her death. Two of Kalenia's sisters contracted the disease and so did her father. We managed to save the girls but my father-in-law passed away a week later.' He trailed off and hung his head, covering his eyes with one hand.

'Woody.' Lorelai caressed his cheek, feeling his pain,

unable to believe the loss he'd suffered. 'So many deaths together. No wonder you understood me so well that first night after John's death. No wonder you stayed and watched over me, taking Hannah when she grizzled so she didn't wake me. You knew how I felt.'

Woody dropped his hand and met her gaze once more. 'She blamed me, Lorelai. Kalenia blamed me for not being able to save our daughter. She was so angry with me, so distraught. My days were dark, my nights were darker, and the point is she was right. I *should* have done more to save Ja'tenya. I should have been vigilant, watched for the symptoms, been able to pre-empt the sickness.'

'You're a doctor, Woody. You're not a miracle worker. I know what it's like to lose someone you love but I cannot even begin to imagine the pain and heartbreak you must have felt at losing your child. I mean, if *anything* were to happen to Hannah, I'd...' Lorelai couldn't even say the words, tears welling in her eyes.

'I wouldn't wish it on anyone.' He cleared his throat and gently eased his hand from hers, rising to his feet. 'Hannah is a wonderful little girl, Lore, and you've done an amazing job of raising her. You should be proud, not only of her but of your own efforts.'

'Thank you, Woody.' She rose, too, knowing he was about to take his leave, the walls having been erected once more. At least he'd taken them down long enough for her to glimpse the darkest moments he'd lived through all those years ago. She was honoured he'd chosen to confide in her.

'I'd best go,' he murmured, and headed towards the entryway closet to retrieve his coat, the mood between them quiet and melancholy. She waited for him to slip his arms into his coat, picking up his cherry-red scarf when it fell to the floor. It seemed so stark and overly bright against his thick woollen coat.

'This fabric is far too cheery right now,' he remarked as he wound the scarf about his neck.

Lorelai forced a smile and reached out to smooth down one side of the scarf that had rumpled. 'I think it suits you. It makes the blues of your irises stand out, highlights your chiselled jaw, your five-o'clock shadow, your manly shoulders.' She let her hand trail down the scarf to the end and was about to clasp her hands together when Woody took hers in his yet again.

'Thank you, Lore.' He raised her hand to his lips, pressing a gentle kiss to her skin. 'I do feel better for having talked some of this out with you.'

'I'm here to listen any time you need me.' She smiled brightly at him. 'That's what friends are for.'

'We *are* friends. Aren't we? I mean, *real* friends.' He shook his head, annoyed with himself for stumbling over the words.

'Good friends,' she agreed.

'Close friends,' he added, and she nodded.

'Yes.'

He looked down at her hand, still enclosed within his. Her light floral scent blending with the lingering aromas from dinner made Lorelai seem definitely good enough to eat. He clenched his jaw as his gaze dipped from her eyes to encompass her mouth, watching as her tongue slipped out to wet her pretty pink lips. Lips that tasted so good, lips that fitted so perfectly against his own, lips he'd dreamed of every night.

He knew how wonderful it had been to kiss another woman, to once again feel those first tingling sensations, the ones that seem to start in your fingertips, spreading up your arm before bursting forth like fireworks throughout your entire body. He knew how ardently she could respond to his touch, the sighing of her body as their souls danced seeming to fit so perfectly against one another.

The need to hold her now, to slip his arms about her waist, to draw her close, feel the warmth of her body next to his, was starting to become overwhelming. She'd somehow managed to get him to really open up and talk about his past. She hadn't offered bland platitudes, she hadn't brushed his feelings aside. Instead, she'd listened and she'd understood. She'd offered compassion and empathy and he felt a weight lift from his shoulders. The burden of carrying so much pain could easily destroy a man but tonight he'd been able to speak freely to a woman who somehow understood him, sometimes better than he understood himself.

'*Close* friends.' Lorelai edged a little closer, wanting the distance between them to vanish. 'Woody,' she whispered. 'I don't want to wreck this new-found friendship but...' she breathed out, her heart rate increasing as the essence of him wound its way around her '...I can't stop thinking about you. The attraction between us has only increased since that morning at Martha's farm and I...want you.'

She closed her eyes, unable to believe she was speaking these words out loud but at the same time feeling liberated in telling him how she truly felt. 'I want you to be around me, around Hannah, to spend time with us.' Opening her eyes, she looked directly into his, her voice strengthening with determination to make him see just what he'd come to mean to her. 'I want to get to know you even more than I do now, to support you in all aspects of your life.'

Woody put his hands on her shoulders, unsure

whether to keep her at a distance or to draw her closer. He couldn't believe what she was saying and he knew he was fortunate to hear those words from her lips. It was clear she really did care about him, just as he cared about her. He, too, wanted to spend time with her, to come around more often, to read stories to Hannah, to simply sit and talk, all snuggly and warm by the heater on a cold and frosty night.

'Lorelai. You are an incredible woman.'

She tried not to show the pain that pierced her soul the instant he spoke those words. 'But you don't feel the same way.' She lowered her gaze and went to step back, to put some much-needed distance between them, but Woody's hold on her shoulder tightened a little, keeping her where she was.

'I didn't say that. You *are* an incredible woman. Full stop. There are no ifs, buts or maybes about that statement. It's completely true.

'Then what are you saying, Woody?' With a heavy sigh she spun on her heel, breaking his hold on her. 'I keep getting completely mixed signals from you. First you keep your distance, then you draw me in with your sexy eyes and irresistible mouth and make me feel like I haven't felt in—well, *for ever,* and then you kiss me before putting me back at arm's length and walking off again. I can't do this, Woody.'

'Lore, I—'

'I understand about your wife. I'm not asking you to forget her. I'm not asking you to confess undying love to me.' She stood in the middle of the room and held her arms out wide. 'I just want to know where I stand with you. I've told you how I feel. If you don't feel the same way, if all you've been doing with me the entire time you've been in town is messing with my mind, then...'

Her voice broke on the last word and she couldn't believe she'd let herself get so worked up she felt like crying.

Woody crossed to her side and without hesitation took her into his arms. Lorelai buried her face in his chest, breathing in his scent and allowing his warmth to wash over her. 'I'm not usually so fragile,' she murmured, sniffing then blinking her eyes a few times in order to get herself under control. 'It's just with John cheating on me—and not just with the woman who was in the car crash with him but I've since found out there were several others before her. Ever since the first day we met, he'd always had another woman on the side. All through our engagement and our marriage. Do you have any idea how it feels? To be so betrayed by someone who professed to love, honour and cherish you?' She eased back, wishing he'd let her go.

'Lorelai. I can't stay in Oodnaminaby. I have—'

She sighed, closing her eyes and shaking her head. 'It's fine. You don't have to explain. I get the point. You can't get seriously involved with me because you're leaving Ood at the end of your contract. You might not be back for years and years because you have a completely different life to live from the one that I live here, in my sleepy little town with my headstrong little girl. I get it.'

She tried to control her voice as she spoke, tried to be strong and brave just as Woody thought she was, yet she couldn't help the little waver that quivered through her voice near the end. She wasn't strong. She didn't want him to go. Even having him here tonight, helping her with Hannah, doing her dishes, making her a cup of tea—all those little things meant so very much to her, especially when she was on her own. Day in, day out, it was just Hannah and herself, going through their daily grind. They'd been doing well, enjoying their life until Woody had come back to town and shown them what their lives were missing…they were missing *him*.

He belonged with them. She felt it to the very depths of her soul and yet here she was, telling him she understood, knowing that he had a different life somewhere else, living in a different place, travelling and helping and doing different things with different people—people who couldn't possibly understand him the way she did.

'Do you, Lore? Do you really get it? Do you understand that you drive me to distraction? Do you comprehend that I'm bad news for you? Do you really think I'd run the risk of hurting you again after what that creep did to you?' His words were vehement and coloured with confused pain. 'You deserve so much better, Lore. You deserve to be treated like a queen. Can you even begin to fathom how painful it is to stand here, holding you in my arms, desperately wanting to kiss you but knowing if I do, I could risk emotionally damaging both of us for ever?' He shook his head. 'Life isn't that simple, Lore.'

'I know, Woody. Don't you think I don't know that?' She wriggled in his arms. 'Let me go. Please let me go or…'

'Or what? Do something crazy? Crazy, like this?'

And with that Woody gave them both what they craved and pressed his lips firmly to hers.

CHAPTER NINE

His lips were soft and gentle on hers and she opened her mouth willingly, her need for him mounting with every passing second. Woody stroked his hands across her face, gently making their way around to the back of her neck where he gently pulled the band from her hair, allowing the blonde strands to fall loose around her face. Tingling with anticipation, his fingers sifted through her silky locks, loving the feel of them. Being this close to her, being allowed to touch her, to press butterfly kisses to her cheeks, to nuzzle her neck, to experience all those sensations he'd only fantasised about was better than any dream. The *real* Lorelai was literally taking his breath away.

When he broke his mouth free, she couldn't help but gasp in air, all the while wanting his mouth back on hers. He continued to wreak havoc on her emotions, flooding her body with wave after wave of goose-bumps and sparkles, with his tiny kisses to her neck, her ear, her cheek before returning to capture her lips with his once more.

This was no testing kiss, not like the first one they'd shared. This time he seemed intent on really delving into her being, to unlock the secrets she kept hidden deep down, almost desperate to know everything about her. Was that because there would never be a repeat of this moment? Was this the last time she'd ever have the opportunity to kiss him?

Desperation flared within her and she slid her hands beneath his coat, tightening her hold around his waist, wanting him to know that she never wanted these exquisite sensations to end. Her heart was bursting with joy and pain and power, so that when she decided to deepen the kiss even further, she was elated when he followed.

His masterful mouth continued to drug her senses. Emotions seemed to swamp her, one after the other, and she wanted them, she welcomed them. In his arms, with his lips firmly on hers, their torsos pressed together, she felt more alive than she'd ever felt before.

She slid her hands lightly over his polo shirt, edging down until she found the end of the material before boldly putting her hands beneath, instantly delighting not only as her fingertips made contact with the hard muscles of his back but also in the way Woody groaned with satisfaction. To know he was as much into her as she was into him gave her hope. Where she'd wondered whether he really felt the same way, his actions were now telling her loud and clear just how much he desired her.

Cherished. Feminine. Sexy.

Woody made her feel all those things and she loved it. No man had ever made her feel this way. No matter what might happen in the future, Woody was her one and only, her true love—for ever.

He broke his mouth free from hers, both of them panting wildly as he buried his face in her neck, breathing in the scent of her hair. It was so amazing to finally be able to give in to his desire to touch her this way. To have the silky strands of her hair brush lightly against his face as he nuzzled her neck.

'Lorelai,' he breathed, her name a caress upon his lips, her hands still splayed over the warm, firm muscles of his back. 'I shouldn't be doing this. I shouldn't be leading you on but you're just too hard to resist.'

'Then don't. Don't resist me,' she whispered against his mouth, pressing another kiss to his lips before he said anything else. 'I know there are obstacles in our way, Woody, but please let me have these moments. I'm going to need to have something to keep me warm on the long and lonely nights after you've left Ood.'

He opened his mouth to say something but she kissed him again. 'Shh. Later.' Closing her eyes, she held him near, resting her ear to his chest, sighing as she listened to the beat of his heart and how she had been the one to make it thump so wildly against his chest. At least she now knew he *did* find her attractive, that he *did* want her as much as she wanted him, and whilst she desperately needed to know what was holding him back, for now, in this one glorious moment, Lorelai felt content.

They stood there for a good five minutes, neither one speaking but both absorbing as much of each other as possible. 'We can't say here for ever,' Woody finally murmured.

'I wish we could,' she returned, but knew he was right. Closing her eyes, she breathed in his essence once more, desperate to commit every aspect of these moments to memory.

'So do I.' He breathed in, her scent firmly wrapped around him, and he loved it. 'I want things to be different, Lore. I really do,' he murmured, his deep tone rumbling through her. 'If you only knew how complicated my life is, perhaps you'd help me to keep my distance.'

Lorelai eased back and looked at him. 'Then tell me, Woody. Open up to me. Share with me this great burden that seems to be weighing you down so heavily that you feel there's absolutely no possible way we could ever be together. Tell me. Please?'

He closed his eyes. 'I can't tell you.'

'Why not?'

'You'll hate me.'

'Impossible.'

He laughed without humour. 'You've hated me before now.'

'No. Never hate, Woody. Perhaps I was annoyed that you wouldn't talk to me, that you felt you couldn't share things with me. We're so in tune with each other. Don't you feel it?'

'I do. I *do* feel it but—' He stopped. Could he do it? Could he tell her about the responsibilities of his world? Tell her of the burden he would have to continue to carry for goodness only knew how many years, to provide for Kalenia's family? How he couldn't leave them in the lurch? How doing his duty was stopping him from finding happiness with her? Could he do it? Would she truly understand?

'Lorelai.' He started to release her from his arms. 'Perhaps we should sit do—'

Lorelai's phone rang, cutting him off. She closed her eyes and hung her head for a moment, unable to believe the bad timing of whoever was phoning her. 'I need to get that,' she murmured, and he instantly dropped his arms, letting her go.

'Of course you do.'

She glanced at the clock on the wall, which read

half past nine, as she headed for the phone. 'A call at this hour is never good news. Dr Rainbow,' she said after she'd connected the call. 'Hello?' she said a moment later, frowning as all she heard was deep, rasping breathing.

'What is it?' Woody asked, concern filling him.

'A heavy breather.'

'In Oodnaminaby? This place is wilder than I thought.'

'Hello?' she tried again.

'Lore?' Her name was squeezed out followed by a groan of pain but that one word was enough for her to identify the person on the other end of the phone. She felt the blood drain from her entire body.

'*Dad*?' His name was a horrified whisper.

'Lore?' BJ said again and this time she heard it more clearly, the inability to get air into his lungs.

'Lorelai?' Woody closed the distance between them and took the phone from her trembling hand. 'BJ?' His firm voice carried down the line.

'Woo—' BJ couldn't even finish his words.

'Where are you?' Woody asked. 'Are you at home?'

'Ye—'

He didn't even need to finish the word. 'I'm calling an ambulance. Lore and I will be there as fast as we can. Try and stay as still as possible, be calm. We're on our way, BJ. Hang in there.'

Woody disconnected the call, then looked at Lorelai who was standing there, clearly in a state of disbelief. 'Lore, who looks after Hannah when you have emergencies?' He was already tapping in the number for the paramedics at Tumut, hoping they weren't out on another call.

'Lorelai?' He snapped his fingers in front of her face,

then put his hand on her shoulder and gave her a little shake. The way she looked was reminiscent of the night John had died and his heart instantly ached for her. She'd already lost so many people, so many who were close and important to her, and the thought that she might now lose her dad was more than her mind could process. 'Snap out of it, honey. I need you here with me. We need to go and save BJ. You and me. We can do this. We can save him.' His words were firm, imploring and filled with determination. 'Who looks after Hannah?'

He had no time to press her further as the paramedics answered his call and he quickly gave them the few details he had. When he'd disconnected, he hauled Lorelai close and pressed his mouth to hers in a swift, harsh kiss, hoping the firm action would be enough to snap her out of wherever she was. 'Lore?'

'Huh?' She blinked rapidly and shook her head, looking unseeingly at him for a brief moment before clarity began to return. 'Babysitter. Right. Edward and Honey are away, so that leaves Connie. I'll call her.' She accepted the phone, then pointed to her mobile phone on the table. 'Call Andrew Paddington. His number's in my phone. He's dad's closest neighbour. He can go around and sit with Dad until we get there. Also, my emergency bag is in the entryway cupboard. Give it the once-over and let me know if we need to stop at the clinic to get anything else.' She turned her attention to the phone as her friend answered. 'Connie? I've got an emergency and Hannah's asleep. Are you or Hank able to...?' A pause, then, 'Thanks. I'd appreciate it.'

Woody was on the phone with Andrew whilst checking her bag as Lorelai headed to her room to quickly change her clothes and put on some shoes, ready for the wintry night before them. She looked out the window and saw it had started to snow again. Her father's house was a good ten minutes from Ood and that was in fine weather. Still, if they took their time, letting the all-wheel-drive do its work, they should reach him in fifteen minutes. Staying calm and focused was of paramount importance. Thank goodness Woody was here, not only in town but with her. If she'd been alone when that call had come through, she might still be standing there in a complete daze.

Lorelai couldn't even begin to contemplate what might happen if they didn't get to her father in time. They had to. They just had to, that was all there was to it. Her dad. Her wonderful, brilliant, funny and fantastic father couldn't be taken from her. She wouldn't allow it.

Tiptoeing into Hannah's room, she bent and kissed her daughter on the forehead, brushing the fine blonde hair back with her fingers. 'I love you, Hannah Emily. Sleep sweet.' As she turned to head out, she saw Woody standing in the doorway, watching her with Hannah. Lorelai was both pleased and surprised when he, too, came quickly into the room and dropped a kiss to Hannah's sleepy head.

He straightened and turned to face her. 'Ready?' he asked, as both of them heard the front door opening, indicating Connie had arrived.

Lorelai nodded and Woody could see that firm determination in her eyes. 'Let's go and save my dad.'

Less than ten minutes after receiving BJ's call they were in their car and on their way to his place, Lorelai unable to sit still as she shifted and fidgeted her worry away. 'It's all well and good telling myself to be professional, to remain calm and collected because I know that's the best way to help my dad at the moment,' she told Woody as he drove her car, following her directions. 'But I'm completely freaking out!'

'That's understandable,' he replied. 'Quite natural, in fact, and perhaps admitting that to me will help you deal with the swirling multitude of emotions currently churning throughout your body and mind.'

'Perhaps.'

They'd stopped at the clinic on the way so Woody could collect a portable oxygen concentrator. 'If he's having trouble breathing, this is the one piece of equipment we'll most definitely need.'

'I just wish I knew what he'd done, why he can't breathe. Is he trapped under something heavy? Is he hurt in some way? How long has he been injured?' Lorelai thumped a fist to the dashboard. 'I hate not knowing my parameters.'

Woody did his best to reassure her whilst concentrating on roads that were now covered with slush and snow. He wanted to do everything he could to help Lorelai in any way possible. He was also surprised at just how concerned he was for her father. It wasn't surprising, given BJ had instantly welcomed him to Oodnaminaby. The man was the rock of the entire mixed Rainbow-Goldmark clan.

BJ had cared for his daughter when his wife had passed away, he'd held the Goldmark boys together after the deaths of their parents and he'd supported his daughter after the death of her husband. Tragedy had been a part of this man's life, a part of his daughter's life, and Woody knew he would do everything in his power to ensure BJ made it, but he could give Lorelai no guarantees.

The fact that Woody had definite feelings for the woman beside him, feelings that no matter how hard he tried to quell them, to push them away, to do everything he could *not* to give into them, meant this case was different from the usual ones he dealt with.

Woody had been in love with Kalenia and yet he'd been unable to save his own daughter. For years he'd carried his wife's harsh words with him, hearing her blaming him for Ja'tenya's death. *'You could have done more. You should have been watching for the signs. It's all your fault she's dead.'*

Once again, the pressure was high and he needed to be vigilant, to check and double-check, to pre-empt, to think quickly. He had no idea what they might find when they went inside the cabin but he fervently hoped his mind would remain sharp and focused.

He glanced across at Lorelai and quickly took her hand in his. 'How are you holding up?'

'Uh…I um…I don't know.'

'You'll be fine. You'll be able to focus. He's your dad. You love him and we're going to do everything we can, Lore. OK? I'm right here with you, working together. We work well together.'

His words, his deep rich voice was working its magic, calming her down, helping her head to come out of the clouds. 'Yes. Yes, we do.'

'See? We'll get BJ sorted out.' He gave her hand one final squeeze before he turned the wheel, bringing the car to a stop outside the front of the small log cabin, which was situated on twenty acres. There were a few cars parked near the front of the house.

'That's Andrew's car. Good. He made it.' Relief crossed Lorelai's face. 'At least Dad's not alone.'

'Right. Let's move,' he said the instant he'd switched

off the engine. 'Lore, you take the medical bag, I'll get the oxygen.' Not waiting for an answer, he opened the car door, eager to get their equipment out and into the house to find out exactly what was going on. Lights seemed to be on everywhere, blazing bright as they headed up the front steps into the house.

'Dad?' she called loudly. 'Andrew? Andrew, where is he?' Even as she spoke, Woody could hear the veiled panic in her tone.

'Through here. Kitchen,' Andrew called. 'I've just checked on the ambulance. They'll be here in ten minutes.'

'Oh, Dad!' Lorelai choked back a sob the instant she saw her father lying on the kitchen floor, rasping for breath, Andrew sitting beside him.

Woody brought the oxygen cylinder with him and quickly knelt down, placing the non-rebreather mask over BJ's mouth and nose before adjusting the dosage. 'There you go, mate. That's going to help.'

Lorelai was beside her father, and when he looked at her she could clearly see panic in his eyes. As she looked at him lying there, for one split second the world seemed to stop turning. When her mother had died, she had been young and there had been nothing she could do. With Hannah and Cameron Goldmark, they'd been cruelly taken from her by an avalanche. In that frozen moment Lorelai realised something—she had the power to save her father. The realisation gave her courage and cleared her mind from the fog surrounding it.

'It's OK, Dad. Everything's going to be fine.' Her words were firm, reassuring and filled with hope. She took out her stethoscope. 'I'm just going to listen to your chest.' She closed her eyes and concentrated on listening. A moment later she frowned. 'This isn't an asthma or panic attack, as I'd initially thought,' she stated, directing her words to Woody. 'There are no breath sounds on the right side. There's also increased hyper-resonance.'

'Pneumothorax?' Woody's eyes widened and he glanced up to look at Lorelai.

'But how? Dad, did you hurt yourself? Fall over? Hit yourself in the chest in some way?'

'Slipped on ice,' BJ gasped, his words intermittent. 'Hit chest on fence post.'

Lorelai rubbed her hands together, trying to warm them before putting them onto her father's chest, carefully checking his ribs. 'Why didn't you call and tell me earlier? Your lung is collapsing, Dad,' she told him. 'But don't you worry because we're going to sort you out. Isn't that right, Woody?'

'Absolutely. You're in luck, BJ, because after my many years working in the jungles of Tarparnii, I've become what the natives call a "bitsa" doctor, because I can do "bitsa this" and "bitsa that", and I've treated several collapsed-lung patients before.' While Woody spoke, he was pulling different things from the medical bag—tubing, a needle, a sterile bandage, a valve. 'Andrew,' he said, looking across at BJ's neighbour, 'I need a bottle with some water in it. Can you find one, please?'

'Wha—?' BJ asked from beneath the oxygen mask.

'What's happening?' Woody asked the question he could see in BJ's eyes. Lorelai was taking the tubing out of the protective wrapper and attaching the valve and needle as Woody spoke. 'BJ, it looks as though your lung has collapsed. That's why you can't breathe properly. There's a collection of air between the chest wall and the lung—the pleural cavity,' Woody said. 'When you fell and hit your chest, that caused a sort of puncture to your lung and now, whenever you breathe out, some of the air is going into the pleural cavity. That's why it hurts so much but, rest assured, we'll have you fixed in a jiffy.'

'That's right,' Lorelai continued. 'And once we've re-established the negative pressure within the cavity, the lung will expand again and everything will be...' She shrugged '... perfect.' She leaned forward and pressed a kiss to her father's forehead.

Andrew came back with the bottle of water, which Woody gratefully accepted. 'Sorry there's no time for an anaesthetic,' he said to BJ, 'but you'll feel better very soon.' He glanced up and met Lorelai's gaze as she handed him the scalpel. 'Are you OK?'

'Oh, yes. Let's save my dad.'

Woody smiled and nodded before making a small incision into the pleural space. He inserted the catheter through the second intercostal space, which would remove the air. The other end of the tube went down into the bottle of water, forming a water seal.

Once that was done, Lorelai assisted as they covered the wound with an airtight dressing. The pressure in BJ's lungs started to change, Lorelai pressing her stethoscope to her father's chest to confirm. 'Hyperresonance decreasing. Nice. That'll hold him until we can get him to Tumut hospital.'

BJ's breathing increased and Lorelai relaxed onto the floor beside her father, relief flooding through her. Her dad was going to be all right—thanks to Woody. She looked across at him to find him watching her closely.

'He's going to be just fine.' His words were sure and steadfast.

'Yes.' She smiled back, her heart filled with gratitude. Woody was a man who had proved himself time and again to be dependable, supportive and thoughtful. She wasn't sure what he'd been about to tell her before her father had rung through and right now she realised it didn't matter.

Her heart most certainly belonged to him.

When the ambulance arrived, Woody insisted that Lorelai ride alongside her father whilst he drove behind in her car. At Tumut hospital the night staff were astonished to learn of BJ's condition, all vowing to look after the State Emergency Services captain to the best of their abilities.

'Of course. Your dad would have worked with most of these people over the years,' Woody stated after the makeshift drain had been replaced. Lorelai sat by BJ's beside, holding his hand while he slept.

'He's certainly saved a lot of lives,' Lorelai agreed. 'And tonight you saved his.'

Feeling choked with emotion, she stood and crossed to where he stood at the foot of the bed. Not caring who saw, she put her arms around his waist, holding him close. 'Thank you, Woody.' She buried her face in his chest. 'Thank you,' she said again, the words muffled against his shirt.

'Lore, you don't have to thank me.'

She eased back and looked at him. 'Oh, yes, I do. I now understand why patients often go on and on about thanking us for the work we do. Of course, being the calm, modest people we doctors are, we nod politely and smile, saying "It was nothing" or "It's my job" or "It's what I've been trained to do". However, I really mean this, Woody. From my heart. You've saved my father's life and I can never repay you or say thank you enough. You understood just how much my father meant to me and you used those clever hands of yours and that amazing intelligent brain to save his life.'

Woody tightened his hold on Lorelai, happy to have her in his arms once again. It felt so perfect to have her near, to have her close to his heart. He gathered her to him and closed his eyes as she rested her head against his chest. It felt right to be like this with her. His heart was beating out a rhythm that he knew was in sync with her own. They belonged together and he felt it with every fibre of his being—yet he knew it could never happen.

His world was different from the happy life filled with sunshine that Lorelai lived here in Ood with her daughter and the rest of her surrogate family. It wasn't that he didn't love Tarparnii and the people who needed him there, it was simply the fact that he didn't get to choose. His path had been carved out during tragedy and he was honour bound to fulfil it.

It was purely selfish of him to be holding Lorelai like this, selfish of him to want more, to have her lips pressed to his yet again, to feel the lightness only she could inject into his world. It would be best if he made a clean break, if he just told her the truth, confessed why he could never be with her, could never have a life with her and Hannah here in Oodnaminaby, and once he told her, she would understand why they needed to fight harder to keep their distance.

With a sigh filled with regret Woody eased back and looked down into Lorelai's upturned face. He wanted to tell her now but she'd already had enough to deal with tonight. Thankfully, BJ had managed to pull through and was now sleeping soundly, well on the way to making a full recovery.

What she needed now was not to bear his burdens but to head home and be with her daughter. He looked into her eyes, the pupils wide in the dim light, the blue of her irises rimming them. She was stunning. Gorgeous. Feminine. Utterly beautiful. *His* Lorelai. Although it was wrong, although he'd tried hard to fight it, there was no denying her importance to him.

His gaze dipped to encompass her lips and when her tongue slipped out to wet them, he couldn't help the groan that escaped from deep within.

'Woody?'

'Lore, you are…exquisite.'

'You're not so bad yourself.' Those tantalising lips of hers curved into an alluring smile, one he found impossible to resist. 'Kiss me, Woody,' she breathed. 'I need you.'

And heaven help him but he needed her, too. Without another word he lowered his head and tenderly captured her mouth with his own.

There were no two ways about it. He knew he shouldn't be kissing Lorelai. He knew he should be keeping his distance not only from her but from her daughter as well. He knew all of this, he knew the logic behind the decision, but whenever he was close to her, he was finding it increasingly difficult to keep from touching her.

There was a connection of their hearts, their souls and their minds, so powerful and strong, drawing him to her, the need pulsing wildly between them. It didn't help his self-control when he knew her kisses were heavenly, intense and powerful. The real Lorelai soft and pliant in his arms, responding to his mouth on hers was infinitely better than a dream. It had been a long time since he'd felt so comfortable, so natural, so light-hearted around a woman that keeping his hands off her was becoming impossible. Lorelai was an incredible woman and he counted himself privileged at her response to his need.

Her want for him was evident and he didn't take it for granted, honoured by her attention. He knew he didn't deserve it, not when at some point in their near future he'd be forced to break not only her heart but her daughter's as well.

He was a man caught between two worlds and right at the moment, as Lorelai responded so ardently to his touch, to the way their mouths seemed to move in an uncanny synchronicity, he chose this world. Staying with Lorelai and Hannah, never having to leave them, never having to hurt them, was what he wanted more than anything.

Unfortunately, he knew it could never be. He was honour bound elsewhere and would be for the rest of his life. He'd been raised to do what was right, what was honourable, and he would fulfil his duty at the expense of his own happiness.

'Lore?' he began, pulling his mouth from hers, needing to talk to her, to tell her the truth about his situation. Earlier in their friendship he hadn't felt it necessary to lay his problems at her feet, preferring to keep them a private matter between himself and those involved. Now, though, with the escalation of his desire for her and his apparent lack of self-control, Woody knew he owed her the truth. It was far better for her to hear it from him rather than someone else.

'Lore?' he tried again, but her answer was to draw his mouth back to hers, desperate to continue kissing him. If he didn't talk, if he simply kept on kissing her, then she wouldn't have to face the future. Right here, right now, in this one moment in time, she was happy.

Her father was improving, her daughter was safe and the man of her dreams, the man she'd been waiting for her entire life, was holding her in his arms, cherishing her with his mouth, protecting her with his heart.

'Lore?' This time he leaned back. 'We need to talk, sweetheart.'

Lorelai shook her head and put her finger over his lips. 'Shh. I don't want to decipher this, Woody. I just want to feel and you most definitely make me *feel*.' She pressed her mouth to his once more, eager to capture his full attention. 'For too long I felt useless and unwanted and unloved but you've changed all that. You make me feel…fantastic and desirable and alive.' Her words were punctuated with kisses, her hands cupping his face ensuring he remained right where he was. 'There'll be time to talk…later.'

Woody knew he should argue, should make her see reason, but it was nigh impossible when he wanted exactly the same thing as her. He moaned in appreciation as he gathered her close, accepting her mouth, wanting to lose himself in her just as much as she wanted to lose herself within him. As the kiss began to intensify, their hearts continued to intertwine. There would be rocky times ahead but the memory of this time, of the two of them together, locked in mutual desire and need for each other, was what would get them through.

'That's a great sight to wake up to,' BJ murmured, and it was only then that Lorelai remembered their location. She slid her arms from Woody at the same time he released her, both of them crossing to BJ's bedside to check on their patient.

'How are you feeling, Dad?' she asked, taking BJ's hand in hers.

'Much better for seeing you with Woody,' he rasped,

speaking slowly. 'It's about time you two kids realised how good you are together.'

Lorelai glanced across at Woody, feeling a little self-conscious at being caught by her father. Woody smiled but she noticed it didn't meet his eyes. Her stomach churned in knots as she realised her present happiness would be short-lived. Woody had something important he needed to discuss with her and whilst she didn't particularly want to hear it, she knew it was inevitable. For now, though, she turned her concentration towards her father and bent to kiss his cheek.

'Don't you ever scare me like that again, you hear?'

'Yes, darling. I won't be going anywhere, especially if there's a big family event coming up.' He winked at her and Lorelai couldn't help the embarrassment she felt at his assumption.

'Well you rest.' She spoke quickly, trying to cover over her father's implication that she and Woody would be getting married soon. 'I'll bring Hannah in to see you tomorrow so you'd best be looking your dapper best.'

'Will do, love.'

Lorelai bent to kiss his cheek again. 'Sleep well and don't tease the nurses.' She pointed her finger at him in a stern manner, using her best 'mother' voice to discipline him.

BJ closed his eyes, showing how even a little exertion could tire him out. 'You spoil all my fun,' he murmured, before his breathing evened out.

Satisfied her father was now doing well, Lorelai turned to Woody. 'Ready to go?'

Woody held out her car keys. 'You go. Be with Hannah. I'm going to stay here a while longer and monitor your dad.'

Alarm instantly flooded Lorelai. 'Why? But…he's

doing really well. I've read his chart.' She pointed to her dad. 'Is there something you're not telling me?'

Woody chuckled and cupped her face in his hands. 'Everything's fine. I just need to…stay. To watch over him. Make sure his progress continues.' He shrugged. 'That's all. Go and get some rest. Cuddle Hannah.'

Lorelai watched him for a moment, recalling something he'd said earlier that night…something about not being vigilant enough where his wife and daughter had been concerned. 'My dad's doing great and he's surrounded by staff who are not only highly trained but care for him on a personal level. He'll be fine.'

'I know. I would like to stay but I'll walk you to the car.'

Lorelai nodded and said goodnight to the staff before heading out. Woody slipped his arm about her waist as they walked side by side, needing her close.

'Woody, you don't need to punish yourself for not being able to save your daughter,' she said softly as they made their way through the quiet hospital. 'My dad will be fine, thanks to you.'

'Exactly, and he's going to stay that way. You've already lost far too many people, Lorelai, and I need to stay here, to be vigilant, to be one hundred per cent sure BJ's not going to develop any further complications. I've learned my lessons the hard way and I'm determined to protect the people I care about.'

Lorelai stopped just before the door and turned to face him. 'You care about me?'

'Oh, honey. I care about you so very much. It's why I need to stay.'

Lorelai reached up and stroked a hand down his determined jaw. 'Your daughter's death wasn't your fault, despite what your wife might have said. You can't keep punishing yourself, Woody.'

He nodded and captured her hand in his, bringing it to his lips. 'You're right. Logically I know Kalenia was only speaking from intense hurt and I *did* do everything possible to save my daughter.'

'Of course you did. Seeing you with Hannah has shown me just how caring and nurturing you are. You would have been an amazing father and I'm sure your baby felt your love.' She smiled at him. 'You're a dynamic man, Woody.'

'Lore.' He gathered her into his arms again and held her. 'Why is it you know just what to say to get through to me?'

'We're connected,' she replied, before leaning up to brush a sweet kiss across his lips. 'I do appreciate you staying, though. Having you here, keeping watch over my dad, it does give me that extra level of security.'

Woody smiled and together they headed out, surprised to find snow had fallen again, making everything look fresh and brilliant and new. He held the door for Lorelai as she climbed into the vehicle, adjusting the seat. He kissed her once, twice before forcing himself to close the door and watch her drive away.

Finding happiness and peace in Lorelai's arms, finally taking those steps to look ahead rather than wishing for the past, had him yearning for a different future. One where he, Lorelai and Hannah made their own family.

He stood there in the snow for a few minutes, watching the flakes float quietly and gently to the ground. Fresh and brilliant and new. If only his life could be that way for ever—but he knew it was impossible.

CHAPTER TEN

'AUNTY Honey!' Hannah squealed with delight, slipping from Woody's lap where the two of them had been sitting down, reading a story together. She ran towards the front door as Honey came inside, Edward not far behind as he hung up the coats.

Lorelai was equally surprised, watching as Honey bent down to welcome Hannah's cuddles.

'What are you doing back so early?' Woody asked as he came over to embrace his sister. 'You've only been gone for just on four weeks.' And those four weeks had been the most confusing and exciting he'd had in so very long. BJ was still in hospital, Woody demanding he stay for at least two days before venturing home. Thankfully, there had been no further complications and Lorelai's father would soon return to full health. The smile he'd seen on Lorelai's face earlier that day when they'd taken Hannah to see her grandfather had warmed his heart. Hannah, of course, had been duly concerned that her granddad was in the hospital but as soon as Lorelai had told the little girl that Woody was looking after granddad, Hannah's brow had cleared and a smile had beamed on her lips.

'Woody can fix him,' she'd stated firmly. 'Woody's the best.' And with that glowing confidence in her beloved Woody, her world had righted itself. Woody had been stunned to have both Lorelai and Hannah having so much faith in him and he had to admit it was an incredible sensation to be so trusted.

Now he smiled as Hannah all but threw herself at her Uncle Edward, his brother-in-law scooping the child up and kissing her neck whilst tickling her. Hannah's giggles filled the room, the glorious sounds of happiness washing over him, warming him all the way through.

'Woody and me was weading,' Hannah told Edward. 'We love weading storwees.' She wriggled from his arms and ran to the sofa to collect the books and show them to her aunt and uncle.

Lorelai embraced her friends, giving them a quick update on her father's excellent progress before making a pot of tea. It was great to have them back, everyone talking at once, a jumble of laughter and happiness. She hadn't realised just how much she'd missed her friends and at the same time she was wary of Honey's natural ability to see right into the heart of people.

Could Honey see that Lorelai was in love with Woody? Was it obvious? Lorelai caught Woody's glance, noting a hint of sadness in his gaze. What did it mean? Now that Honey and Edward had returned, was Woody planning on skipping town again? Leaving as quietly as he had last time? Without even saying goodbye? Her heart began to ache at the thought of him gone, of not seeing him, of not being able to bask in the warmth of his presence, but now was not the time to dwell on it. She pushed the emotions aside for now and pasted on a happy smile.

Soon the four of them were watching as Hannah eagerly unwrapped the cache of presents Honey and Edward had given her.

'We thought you would have been away for much longer,' Lorelai said as she sipped her tea.

'Not that we're not elated at having you home,' Woody added, conscious his sister was watching the interaction between himself and Lorelai very closely. They were sitting together on the sofa, his arm stretched out along the back cushions, Lorelai's body angled towards his, her legs crossed beneath her.

'The travelling became too tiresome,' Honey murmured as she rubbed her belly. 'I feel tired more often, frumpy—'

'You're not frumpy,' Edward quickly interjected, leaning over to kiss his wife.

'Besides, I missed everyone too much. Four weeks was long enough. I don't know why I ever thought I could stay away for longer.'

'Plus the nesting instinct has kicked in and the places we were staying at seemed to take offence when Honey would re-clean the room after the maid.'

Lorelai laughed and smiled at her friend. 'I remember that instinct. It became so strong with me that I actually vacuumed my cutlery drawer.'

Honey laughed. Edward smiled. Hannah oohed at the book she was looking at and Woody found himself wishing *he* had been Hannah's father. He closed his eyes for a moment, imagining a pregnant Lorelai walking around this house, tidying up Hannah's toys, *his* child growing inside her. She would smile at him, welcoming him into her arms. He would kiss her and then kiss her belly, already in love with his unborn child. Pain pierced his heart at the image and he quickly opened his eyes, astonished to find his sister watching him closely.

Honey knew him too well, had practically raised him, and he'd learned at a very young age that trying to hide things from her was plain ridiculous. He tuned his thoughts back into the conversation but only listened with half an ear as Edward recounted an amusing story from their travels.

'Well,' Honey said the moment Edward's tale had finished, 'I have an idea.' She wriggled out of the chair and stood, stretching her back muscles before looking at Hannah. 'How would you like to come and have a sleepover at our house tonight? Uncle Edward has missed your cuddles and kisses and reading you lots and lots of stories.'

Hannah scrambled to her feet and started jumping up and down, clapping her hands with delight. 'Yes. Yes. Yes.' She quickly ran to Lorelai and pleaded with earnest eyes. 'Please, Mummy? Oh, please?'

Lorelai put her cup down on the table and looked at Honey. 'Are you sure? You've only just got home and—'

'And we've both missed her so much, haven't we, Eddie?'

Edward blinked once, obviously having difficulty following his wife's train of thought. He looked into Honey's eyes for a second before his confusion cleared and he nodded. 'Yes. Absolutely. Missed you all but most especially our Hannah cuddles. Now that we're going to be parents soon, we need to get lots of practice cuddling yummy children.'

'Cuddle me. Cuddle me.' Hannah ran to Edward's side and begged to be picked up.

'Well…OK, then. If you're sure.' A little bemused, Lorelai stood. 'I'll go pack her a bag.'

'Tum on, Uncle Edward,' Hannah insisted. 'We choose the storwees.' She urged him to follow her mother and a moment later Woody was left alone with his sister.

'Neatly orchestrated,' he ventured, no stranger to his big sister's tactics of gentle manipulation.

'What's going on, Woody?'

'Why?'

'Because I received a call from K'nai in Tarparnii. Apparently Nilly's been trying desperately to get in contact with you.'

'I know.' Woody closed his eyes and shook his head. 'She wants me to come home for the *par'Mach*.'

Honey thought for a moment. 'That's in about four days' time! Why didn't you call me? Ask me to come back earlier? I thought one of Kalenia's sisters was taking part in the festival? As head of the clan, you need to be there for her.'

'Yes, but I did mention to Nilly before I left that I wasn't sure whether I'd make it back in time. She said she would get another elder to fill in the duties. She said she understood and that helping you was also an honourable cause.' He shook his head and raked a hand through his hair, confusion etched on his brow. 'But lately she's been sending more messages, urging me to come home.'

'Well, now that Eddie and I are back, you're free to go.'

'Free?' He laughed without humour. 'Yeah. I'm free to leave but never free to have the life I want.' His shoulders slumped and he shook his head. Honey watched him for a moment then gasped.

'You haven't told Lorelai?'

'I've told her most of it,' he defended, his hackles starting to rise.

'Woody!' There was censure in Honey's tone and Woody didn't like it. 'She's in love with you.'

'And I'm in love with her,' he replied, then stopped

as though he hadn't expected to say those words out loud. He raised his eyebrows in surprise and stared at Honey, watching the slow smile spread over his sister's face. 'I'm in love with her!' he breathed with a hint of incredulity. 'Wow.'

'Oh, Woody.' Honey hugged her big little brother close. 'You're such a goose. You've always been so intent on protecting everyone else but yourself.' She smiled up at him. 'But I'm very glad to see you didn't protect your heart so fiercely that you locked it away for good. You deserved to be loved, and I can't think of anyone more deserving of you than Lorelai. You'll make a wonderful couple.'

He shrugged. 'No, we won't. We can't have a future together.'

Honey frowned. 'What? Why not?'

'Because of my responsibilities.' He took a step back and spread his arms wide, his tone imploring. 'It's not fair to Lore, Honey. She's been through so much over the years, lost so many people, experienced emotional hardship. I can't ask her to take on my problems. I'd never do that to her, or to Hannah. They both deserve better than I can give.'

'And that makes you sad. Poor Woody.' She smiled up at him, her eyes full of promise. 'As a word of advice, don't go giving up hope and predicting the end too soon. I thought I had no future with Eddie and now look at me.' She stared up into his face. 'I love you, Woody. You're a good man and you'll do what's right. You always do but please don't sell Lorelai short. She's incredible.'

He nodded as he hugged his sister. 'I know and that's the problem. She's so amazing, so great, so...' He exhaled harshly and raked a hand through his hair, knowing it was time to face the music. He'd been on the verge of telling her two nights ago before BJ's emergency. Since then, he hadn't wanted to burden Lorelai with his problems, especially when she was concerned about her dad. However, with Honey and Edward back, there really was no reason for him to miss the *par'Mach* festival and he knew Kalenia would want him to do honour to her sister as well as to her clan.

He nodded with determination. 'I'll talk to her.'

Honey smiled. 'I proud of you, Woody.'

Within another fifteen minutes he was alone in the house with Lorelai. She closed the front door, a look of bewilderment on her face. 'I have no idea what just happened.'

'Honey happened.' Woody shook his head. 'She just...*knows* things. She always has.' He stood by the heater and shoved his hands into his pockets. 'It made it difficult trying to keep her birthday presents a secret.'

Lorelai chuckled and crossed to his side. 'So what does Honey know that resulted in her kidnapping my daughter for the night?'

'She knows I haven't told you the truth.'

At his words Lorelai's mouth instantly went dry and her heart started to pound painfully against her chest.

'What? How can she know that?' And had Honey guessed about Lorelai's feelings for Woody? More than likely, as she was obviously giving them the opportunity to talk things out. Lorelai forced herself to breath calmly, to keep herself under control, even though it appeared Woody was about to tell her what she wasn't at all sure she wanted to hear. He was going to tell her why they could never be together and she didn't want to hear it.

Woody shook his head. 'I've stopped trying to figure out how she can read people, me especially, so easily and just accept that she can.'

Lorelai nodded gently, then closed her eyes, swallowing compulsively over her still dry throat. 'I don't know if I want you to tell me, Woody. I don't want to hear whatever it is you're going to say because I know it'll take you away from me, away from the incredible way you make me feel.' Her heart was hammering fiercely against her chest and her stomach was churning with fear.

'Why don't we sit down?' She could hear the uncertainty in his voice.

'No.' She opened her eyes and stared at him, brushing away a tear from her lashes. 'Just tell me. Blurt it out. Rip the plaster off.' She straightened her shoulders and lifted her chin with a hint of defiance.

Woody's heart pounded with love for the brave, courageous, beautiful woman before him. Her inner strength revealed itself right before his very eyes and he couldn't help but be enamoured by it. Even when faced with a situation she didn't want, she was still incredibly beautiful. His heart churned with love for her.

He exhaled slowly, then nodded. 'OK. Good. That's what I'll do.' He rubbed his hands together and clenched them tight. 'Well, as you know, I was married to Kalenia. She has three younger sisters and no brothers. When we were married, I became the only other male in the family besides her father. In Tarparnii, the males are responsible for providing for their greater clan. Her aunts and cousins live in the village and whilst there are other men around to help with the day-to-day needs, when Kalenia's father passed away, I became head of the clan, so to speak.'

Lorelai listened intently, processing his words carefully and slowly realisation started to sink in. 'You're responsible for them?'

'Yes, and I always will be.'

Her thoughts churned as she processed this information. 'That's why you spend so much time in Tarparnii. Why you're always working a few months here and there but always returning to Tarparnii.'

'Yes. I do love the country. I love the people. I love the beauty and simplicity of life, but travelling and working in other countries for short contracts gives me the opportunity to keep my skills up to date.' Woody paused and dropped his hands back to his sides. 'However, when Kalenia's father passed away, I was determined to do right by her mother and sisters, to accept the responsibility of provider and to be there for them in any way I could.'

'Do you have…?' She shrugged. 'I don't know, official duties of some kind? Rituals? Ceremonies?'

'Yes. I'm required to attend various ceremonies and confer with the other elders in the village about any important decisions throughout the year.' He breathed out slowly. 'I have far too many people relying on me, sometimes waiting for my return so they can make decisions and move on with their lives.'

'How do you keep in contact with them?'

'Post. Satellite phone. An occasional email or phone call via PMA.'

'Ah…the phone calls you've been receiving. You've been called home?'

'Yes. There is a ceremony in a few days' time that I wasn't planning to attend. It had all been sorted out with one of the other elders in the village offering to fill in to complete my duties, but for some reason Kalenia's mother needs me home.' Woody moved away from Lorelai and started to pace.

Lorelai nodded. 'Then you should go.'

'I don't want to. For the first time ever I don't want to return to Tarparnii. These weeks I've been here in Oodnaminaby, spending time with you and Hannah, have been the happiest I've had in a very long time. *You* make me happy, Lore, and I don't want it to end, but—'

'But you already have another family,' Lorelai finished for him, then rubbed her hand across her forehead as she tried to process what he was saying.

'Yes. It's why I was desperate to try and keep my distance from you. Colleagues or friendship was fine but you...' Woody swallowed and stepped forward to take her hands in his. 'You've worked your way into my heart, Lore. Before I met you, I was more than happy to stay in Tarparnii for most of the year, to provide for Kalenia's people, to uphold my promises and respect their traditions. Now I don't want to leave you or Hannah but I must. I am duty bound elsewhere and to break from Kalenia's family now would bring disrespect to her entire clan. Her sisters would never be able to find worthy husbands and her mother would be shunned by others.'

Lorelai bit her lip, trying to control her tears as she realised Woody wasn't free. 'You're already tied to another family.'

'Yes.'

'That is so like you. You have such a strong sense of duty and honour, willing to sacrifice your own happiness for others. You're protecting them, just as you used to protect the other kids in the communes from being picked on in the schoolyard. Just as you protected me in my hour of need—my knight in shining armour.'

'I don't think my armour's all that shiny but on the helping scale, I think the feeling is mutual. You've helped me just as much, Lore. You've helped me let go of the guilt I've carried with me since Ja'tenya's death.' He reached out and brushed the back of his hand across her cheek, a small, sad smile on his lips. 'You're amazing, Lorelai. So strong and determined, so caring and kind.' His tone dropped and he cupped her face, stepping closer, his need for her doubling in that one moment. 'So beautiful and so incredibly sexy.'

Without another word Woody bent and claimed her lips, eager to show her just how much he loved her, how much he wished things were different and how he was incredibly proud of her for being so brave at such a painful time.

Tears ran down her face, their saltiness mingling with the sweet taste from his mouth as she kissed him back, putting all her love into the embrace, wanting to show him that her love for him would never die, no matter what.

When they broke apart, she rested her head against his chest, her tears wetting his shirt. 'You're not mine. You're not mine to have and to hold.' Even as she said the words she clung to him, desperate to somehow change their paths so they could always be together, but she knew it was impossible.

'Make it quick. Like last time,' Lorelai had pleaded. 'Don't say goodbye. It's too...'

'Final,' he'd finished for her before capturing her lips with his once more. As he passed through the jungle terrain, heading for Kalenia's village where his

Tarparniian family was waiting for him, Woody closed his eyes, remembering the feel of Lorelai's mouth on his. They were a perfect fit both physically, mentally and emotionally. In the past, whenever he'd returned to Tarparnii, he'd always felt a sense of homecoming.

This time, though, he felt bound and shackled, even though Nilly and her daughters didn't deserve to be the reason for that sensation. If he left them now, if he self-ishly walked away to pursue a life with Lorelai, he would leave them destitute and in disrespect. There would be no dowries, no opportunities, no promise of a future. Lorelai was right when she'd said he was a protector. He'd always been that way from a very young age and whilst he knew protecting Nilly and her daughters was the right thing to do, Lorelai and Hannah also needed protection.

'Hey. Wake up.' K'nai, his old friend, had brought the jungle Jeep to a stop. 'We are here.'

Woody opened his eyes and looked out at the village he'd called home for such a long time. It was the same. It would never change. Quite a few of the villagers came to welcome him home, speaking rapidly in Tarparnese as they embraced. Woody was happy to see them and forced a smile. He was doing what was right, even though his heart was broken.

'One day!'

Lorelai paced around her lounge room, Honey lying on the sofa with her feet up, Hannah sitting at the coffee table, colouring in.

'He's been gone one day and already I feel as if an enormous part of me is missing.' Lorelai pressed a hand to her heart. 'I can't breathe. I can't sleep. I can't think clearly.' She stopped pacing and spread her arms wide. 'How am I going to concentrate for clinic tomorrow? Poor Edward has returned from holidays and been dumped with weekend duty and a few house calls.'

Honey waved her words away. 'He doesn't mind. He was champing at the bit to get back and connect with his patients. You know Eddie. He loves this town and its people.'

'So do I. But…I love Woody more.'

'Me too,' Hannah piped up. When Woody had said goodbye to the little girl, he'd simply told her he had to go away for a trip, just like Aunty Honey and Uncle Edward had done. He hadn't said how long he'd be gone and Hannah had listened intently before nodding.

'And you'll bring me back lots of presents?' she'd checked. Woody had laughed and promised her a whole sackful of presents as he'd hugged the little girl close, the sight of the two of them piercing Lorelai's heart.

'He belongs with us,' Lorelai continued as she started to pace again. 'The three of us together. Him. Me. Hannah. A family. He had a family before and they were tragically taken from him.'

Honey smiled. 'I'm so glad he's told you about his past.'

Lorelai paused. 'That's right. I remember he said you were in Tarparnii when Ja'tenya was born, that you nursed her back to health.'

'I did what any doting aunt would do. She was gorgeous, Lore.' Honey sighed. 'I wish I could have said something to you about Woody's life, especially when I could see how perfectly the two of you were for each other, but I couldn't.' She shrugged. 'It wasn't my story to tell. I just had to trust that you and my genius brother would work it out in your own way.' Honey nodded with satisfaction. 'So now that you've realised you and Hannah belong with Woody, what are you going to do about it?'

Lorelai stopped and looked at her friend. 'What do you mean? I can't do anything about it.'

'Can't you?'

'Well, short of getting on a plane, flying to Tarparnii and demanding he admit we have some sort of future together—' Lorelai stopped in mid-tirade as her words slowly started to sink in. 'We have some sort of future together.' Her eyes widened as she stared at Honey. 'Why does it have to be all or nothing? Why can't he have both? Why can't *we* have both?' Lorelai started pacing again, although this time it was more thoughtful than frustrated. 'He loves Tarparnii, right?'

'Right.'

'He needs to provide for Kalenia's family, right?'

'Right.'

'So…why can't we provide for them together?'

'Exactly,' Honey remarked as she sat up a little straighter. 'Pass me the phone. We have some organising to do.'

Hannah was incredibly excited to be going on an aeroplane and with her purple and pink backpack proudly on her back, holding onto her mother's hand, they embarked on this new adventure together.

'We get Woody,' she'd told her granddad BJ before they'd left. 'We gonna bring him *home*. We *love* him, don't we, Mummy?'

'Yes,' Lorelai had agreed, sure and firm in her decision. When it had come time to board the plane for Tarparnii, though, she'd started to falter. Honey had convinced her it was best to surprise Woody and had organised for Woody's friend K'nai to meet them at the airport.

'It's all arranged,' she'd told Lorelai. 'Woody will go

completely bug-eyed when he sees you and Hannah.'
Honey had clutched her hands to her chest. 'Oh, I wish
I could be there to see his face!'

Now Lorelai wasn't so sure. Perhaps Woody really
wouldn't want them to encroach on his life in Tarparnii.
Perhaps he wouldn't be happy to see them. Butterflies
of doubt churned in her stomach and if it hadn't been
for Hannah tugging her forward onto the plane, Lorelai
might have chickened out.

'Think about Woody. About how much you love him.
About how much he means to you,' she whispered to
herself as the plane taxied. Hannah was busy looking
out the window, oohing and ahhing at everything she
saw, drinking in the experience and having a wonderful
time. And why shouldn't she be happy? She was going
to find her precious Woody. There was no doubt Woody
would be pleased to see Hannah, he loved Hannah but
what about her? Did he love her? *Really* love her?

Lorelai closed her eyes and tried to calm her thoughts.
It was done now. They were on the plane, the adventure
had begun. Whatever was going to happen was out of
her hands and she'd do well to simply let the fear and
trepidation leave her and join in Hannah's joy.

At the Tarparniian airport they were warmly welcomed by Woody's friend, K'nai, who somehow recognised them immediately.

'Not many people travel with children,' he said as he
carried their luggage to his open-topped Jeep. 'Besides,
I would have recognised you anyway. Woody described
you perfectly.'

'Oh.' Lorelai smiled shyly and blushed a little, although secretly she was pleased Woody had spoken
of her to his old friend. As they drove along, Lorelai

gasped in delight at the lush green scenery spread before her. Everywhere she looked, there were trees.

'Look, Mummy!' Hannah had pointed as Lorelai held her firmly as the only 'seat-belt' was a piece of rope to hold you to the chair. 'A monkey.'

'That is called a *ne'quaha*,' K'nai informed her, and Hannah instantly repeated it, giggling at the sound of the foreign words on her tongue.

'She will be speaking like a native in no time at all.' K'nai laughed. As they drove to the village, they waved a greeting to every passing car. Sometimes K'nai would honk his horn if there was an animal near the edge of the road and it would quickly scuttle out of the way. Twice they stopped to offer a lift to people and by the time they arrived in the village almost forty minutes later, Lorelai was already in love with the place.

'Everyone's so friendly and welcoming and…happy,' she remarked as K'nai helped Hannah from the Jeep. Lorelai bent to pick up Hannah's forgotten backpack. When she straightened, she looked directly into rich, blue eyes…eyes that were wide and bright with surprise.

'Need some help?' His deep, familiar tone washed over her and she felt as though she could breathe easy for the first time since he'd left.

'Woody!'

He held out his hand to help her from the Jeep and the moment she placed her hand in his, she was overwhelmed with a sense of homecoming. She was here. With Woody. *Her* Woody. The man who held her heart and always would.

Their gazes held, both of them drinking in the sight of each other as though it had been years since they'd seen each other rather than just a few days.

'You're here.'

'I'm here,' she repeated, and sighed.

'Why? Why are you here, Lore?'

'Don't you want me to be?' Confusion and panic started to rise within her before her held her close, wrapping his arms around her. She closed her eyes and breathed him in, wanting desperately so much for him to be with her for ever and hoping he'd accept her reasoning for this impromptu trip.

'Oh, Lore.' He rested his chin on her head and breathed in the sweet, fresh scent he always equated with his darling Lorelai.

'I'm here too, Woody. Hug *me*,' Hannah demanded, as she tugged at his trouser leg.

Without releasing Lorelai, Woody bent and scooped Hannah up into his arms. 'Both my girls,' he whispered. 'I must be dreaming.'

Lorelai eased back and raised an eyebrow. 'Your girls?' she couldn't help tease, even though she still wasn't sure he was happy they'd come. Hope flared a moment later when he smiled, a wide beaming smile that for the first time in weeks met his twinkling eyes.

'Don't worry about me,' K'nai said. 'I'll just lug the bags to the hut,' he replied as he headed off.

'Yeah, thanks, mate,' Woody called after his friend. Hannah wriggled from his arms.

'I want to go with K'nai,' she demanded.

'Uh…well…um…' Lorelai looked to Woody for help. 'You know the place better than I do. Will she be all right?'

Woody blinked for a moment, surprised Lorelai was deferring to him as though he really *was* Hannah's father. 'She'll be fine. It's safe.'

Hannah cheered and clapped but Woody's voice held a warning.

'But you stay close to K'nai. OK, princess?'

'Yes, Woody,' Hannah dutifully replied, and within another moment had run off after her new friend.

'He'll watch her, introduce her to his children. She'll be fine,' he promised Lorelai.

'If you say so.'

'You trust me that much?'

'Of course I do.' Lorelai smiled brightly up at the man of her dreams. Woody adjusted his hold on Lorelai, slipping both arms about her waist.

'Why are you here, Lore?'

Lorelai wasn't quite sure how to answer that. Did she confess she was in love with him? Say that Hannah had missed him so much they'd just had to fly all the way to Tarparnii? Tell him she'd come to support him? That she'd only been half a person without him? That even though it had only been a few days since he'd left Oodnaminaby, it had been far too long? Or should she just say she refused to live the rest of her life without him?

Indecision warred through her and she decided the best thing she could do was to show him. Without another word she stood on tiptoe and pressed her mouth to his. Woody obviously approved of her answer as he moaned with delight before deepening the kiss.

Lorelai was here. She'd come after him. Surely that was a good sign? He hadn't been able to stay in Ood and so she'd followed him to Tarparnii. Lorelai was here. He had no idea why but right now he didn't really care. *Lorelai was here.*

The village was larger than she'd imagined, a line of huts with thatched roofs positioned around the edge of a big clearing, a well having pride of place in the centre. Children of all ages ran around the clearing, playing games and laughing. Goats were tethered to the side, eating anything they could.

Next to each hut was a small garden, some growing flowers, most growing vegetables. Women were scattered here and there, tending to the various tasks of food preparation, gardening and stringing long garlands of flowers together, no doubt for the *par'Mach* festival to be held tonight. Young boys were restocking a wood pile and helping with other chores. The whole place was a hive of activity and Lorelai couldn't help but drink it all in.

'It's a different world,' Lorelai breathed as Hannah ran up to them.

'I can run super-fast here in 'Parni,' she told them both. 'Watch me.' And off she ran again.

'Well, she's settled,' Lorelai murmured, and Woody smiled, holding her hand in his.

'Come. There's someone I want you to meet.'

'Who?'

'Nilly. Kalenia's mother. She was called away to the next village and has been gone for the past few days. She only arrived back just before you. I haven't had a proper chance to see her since I returned.'

'I hope every thing's all right,' Lorelai said as Woody directed them towards one of the huts. She stopped him short, just outside the door. 'Wait. Woody, should I be meeting her?'

'What's the problem?'

'Well…us. Whatever this is between us… I…um… don't want her to feel…threatened or something. That I'm trying to take you away from your responsibilities, because I'm not.'

Woody's answer was to squeeze her hand a little tighter. 'Relax. They understand the search for happiness. They're wonderful people, Lore, and I know they'll love you.'

And he was right. Nilly, Kalenia's mother, hugged her close and stroked her blonde hair. 'Shiny,' she replied. 'So beautiful. Your eyes are wise and yet…' She pressed her hand to Lorelai's cheek. 'You have known great sadness, child, just like Woody.'

Lorelai's eyes started to fill with tears at the maternal tone and she forced a smile. 'Thank you for your welcome. Hannah and I are very happy to be here.'

'As are we to have you and your daughter here.' Nilly looked to where Hannah was already joining in with the other children, running about, playing and laughing as though travelling to a different country was something she did every day.

Nilly returned her attention to Woody. 'I am sorry I was not here when you returned. There have been many final arrangements to be made but…' She sighed and smiled. 'They are done.' She smiled at Lorelai. 'We have a big festival tonight. The *par'Mach*. My daughter is to be bonded with her *par'machkai* and she is all…' Nilly paused, searching for a word.

'In a dither?' Lorelai provided, and Nilly nodded.

'Exactly. Now, there is other news I must tell Woody. It is the reason I was so insistent you return for the festival.'

'What's wrong, Nilly? Please tell me.' Woody placed a concerned hand on his mother-in-law's arm but she patted his hand. The smile that lit Nilly's dark eyes and tanned skin was beaming.

'Everything is perfect, my son.' Nilly clasped her hands together. 'A great friend has come to live in our village since you left. He lived in my village when I was a young girl and we were close friends. His name

is Ka'nu and since he has come to be here, we have…'
Nilly stopped and Lorelai could have sworn the other
woman was blushing. 'I am also to take part in the bonding at the *par'Mach*. Ka'nu will be my *par'machkai*.'
Nilly clutched her hands to her chest and Lorelai, even
though she didn't completely understand what was happening, recognised the look of a woman in love.

'What's a *par*…?' Lorelai trailed off, not sure she
could pronounce the word properly.

'It means romantic life partner. Or, in your language,
husband.'

'That's beautiful.' Lorelai smiled at Nilly. 'Congratulations, Nilly.'

Woody was gobsmacked and she had to give him
a little nudge to snap him out of it. 'Uh…Nilly!' He
hugged the small woman close to his chest. 'I can see
that this has made you very happy.'

'It has, my son. Ka'nu has never had a *par'machkai*
before and he is most willing to take on all care of my
daughters within the village. He has become a clear
leader within the village and all that is left is your blessing.'

'My blessing?' He was humbled. 'Nilly, it's yours. If
you have found love again, I am very happy for you.'

'As am I, for you,' Nilly remarked, looking over at
Lorelai with a smile. She held out her hand, beckoning
Lorelai towards her. 'A heart that loves with deep emo-
tion is never lonely. Life is filled with colour.' She took
Lorelai's hand in hers and then placed it in Woody's.
She rested her hand on top. 'I bless your union. Fill it
with colour.'

Woody replied to her in Tarparnese and then trans-
lated for Lorelai. 'We accept your blessing, Mother, and
respect your wise ways.'

Nilly smiled, then looked outside her door. 'I hear the men returning from food gathering. Ka'nu is waiting with impatience to meet you, Woody. I shall collect him. Please wait. I will soon be back.' With a spring in her step Nilly headed out of her hut, pausing to slip on her shoes before crossing the large open area in the centre of the village.

Lorelai and Woody stood in silence for a moment, their hands still entwined as the reality of what Nilly had revealed started to sink in. 'She's getting married again.' Woody spoke slowly then turned to look at Lorelai. 'She's getting married again!'

'What does this mean?'

'It means my obligation to Nilly and her clan is… finished.'

Lorelai's eyes widened in surprise. 'You're no longer responsible for them?'

'No. I'll still love them, I'll still be a part of them and always will be, but…' He slowly exhaled as the truth of the situation hit him. 'I'm free.' He turned to face her, gathering her close. 'I'm free!' He pressed his lips to hers, then laughed out loud. 'I didn't realise what a weight had been on my shoulders.'

Lorelai smiled and rested her hands on those broad shoulders of his. 'But you carried that weight and far more around with you for so long. You're a wonderful man, Woody. So strong and dependable. So honest and caring. So protective and loving. When you left Ood, I couldn't bear it. I couldn't think, I couldn't sleep, I couldn't focus on anything except that you'd gone, you'd left me.'

'Never. I may not have been physically with you but my heart is forever yours, Lore.'

At his glorious words she kissed him again. 'Woody,

the reason I came here, the reason Hannah and I needed to follow you, was because…I love you, Woody. With all my heart, and I didn't want you to feel you had to carry your burdens alone. I wanted to come and tell you that whatever you needed to do to support Nilly and her family, I would stand by you—always.'

Lorelai shook her head, her heart, her eyes, her words filled with love. 'We belong together. You. Me. Hannah. I love the way you care for Hannah, the way you adore your sister and the way you willingly stepped into the role of protector for Nilly and her clan in what was most probably a dark time for you all. I love you, Woody, and I would be honoured if you'd be my *par'machkai*.' She stared up at him, then bit her lip. 'Did I say it right?'

Woody looked at her with a mixed expression somewhere between surprise and elation but hidden in the depths was the smallest hint of doubt. 'You said it perfectly but, Lore, are you sure? Are you sure I'm the man you want?'

'Why wouldn't I want to spend the rest of my life with you, Woody?' There was no hesitation in her tone. She knew, even though he'd never said the words, that he loved both her and Hannah. He'd make the most wonderful father, of that she was sure. He was the man for her and she wasn't about to let any minor hint of doubt ruin that.

'Lore, I…' He shook his head. 'What if I mess things up? Near the end of her life, Kalenia was—'

'Depressed and not in her right mind. Her death, that of your child and your father-in-law were not your fault and I'm sure Nilly and everyone else here in this village would agree with me.' Lorelai clasped both his hands in hers and gave him a watery smile, her voice rich with emotion. 'I'm scared, too, Woody. I failed at my first marriage, remember?'

'You didn't fail. John failed you.'

'Either way, it wasn't a success but with you I know it will be different. Both of us felt that dynamic pull towards each other the first time we met. This—you and I—it's meant to be. I really want you to be my *par'machkai*, Woody. I'm excited to take part in the festival, to learn the customs of the Tarparniian people, to come back and visit Nilly and the rest of the village many times. They're a part of you and therefore they're a part of me. Please, please, say you'll be my *par'machkai*?'

Woody's answer was to bend down and brush a soft kiss across her lips. 'I'd be honoured. I love you, Lorelai. I have for quite some time but I kept thinking I'd lose you so didn't want to offer a commitment.'

'You're nuts.'

'Yes, yes, I am. I'm also crazy—crazy for you. Taking part in the festival tonight will be wonderful, declaring our love in the bonding ceremony.'

'And don't think this lets you off the hook of a bona fide proposal when we return to Australia,' she murmured against his mouth as he kissed her. 'I've proposed here in Tarparnii so it's up to you to propose to me for our Australian wedding.'

Woody smiled down into the face of the woman he loved, unable to believe how happy she made him. 'All right. I'll propose,' he murmured. 'But do you think you'll say yes?'

Lorelai's answer was to laugh before pressing her lips lovingly to his.

* * * * *

Mills & Boon® Hardback

February 2012

ROMANCE

An Offer She Can't Refuse	Emma Darcy
An Indecent Proposition	Carol Marinelli
A Night of Living Dangerously	Jennie Lucas
A Devilishly Dark Deal	Maggie Cox
Marriage Behind the Façade	Lynn Raye Harris
Forbidden to His Touch	Natasha Tate
Back in the Lion's Den	Elizabeth Power
Running From the Storm	Lee Wilkinson
Innocent 'til Proven Otherwise	Amy Andrews
Dancing with Danger	Fiona Harper
The Cop, the Puppy and Me	Cara Colter
Back in the Soldier's Arms	Soraya Lane
Invitation to the Prince's Palace	Jennie Adams
Miss Prim and the Billionaire	Lucy Gordon
The Shameless Life of Ruiz Acosta	Susan Stephens
Who Wants To Marry a Millionaire?	Nicola Marsh
Sydney Harbour Hospital: Lily's Scandal	Marion Lennox
Sydney Harbour Hospital: Zoe's Baby	Alison Roberts

HISTORICAL

The Scandalous Lord Lanchester	Anne Herries
His Compromised Countess	Deborah Hale
Destitute On His Doorstep	Helen Dickson
The Dragon and the Pearl	Jeannie Lin

MEDICAL

Gina's Little Secret	Jennifer Taylor
Taming the Lone Doc's Heart	Lucy Clark
The Runaway Nurse	Dianne Drake
The Baby Who Saved Dr Cynical	Connie Cox

Mills & Boon® Large Print

February 2012

ROMANCE

The Most Coveted Prize	Penny Jordan
The Costarella Conquest	Emma Darcy
The Night that Changed Everything	Anne McAllister
Craving the Forbidden	India Grey
Her Italian Soldier	Rebecca Winters
The Lonesome Rancher	Patricia Thayer
Nikki and the Lone Wolf	Marion Lennox
Mardie and the City Surgeon	Marion Lennox

HISTORICAL

Married to a Stranger	Louise Allen
A Dark and Brooding Gentleman	Margaret McPhee
Seducing Miss Lockwood	Helen Dickson
The Highlander's Return	Marguerite Kaye

MEDICAL

The Doctor's Reason to Stay	Dianne Drake
Career Girl in the Country	Fiona Lowe
Wedding on the Baby Ward	Lucy Clark
Special Care Baby Miracle	Lucy Clark
The Tortured Rebel	Alison Roberts
Dating Dr Delicious	Laura Iding

ROMANCE

Roccanti's Marriage Revenge	Lynne Graham
The Devil and Miss Jones	Kate Walker
Sheikh Without a Heart	Sandra Marton
Savas's Wildcat	Anne McAllister
The Argentinian's Solace	Susan Stephens
A Wicked Persuasion	Catherine George
Girl on a Diamond Pedestal	Maisey Yates
The Theotokis Inheritance	Susanne James
The Good, the Bad and the Wild	Heidi Rice
The Ex Who Hired Her	Kate Hardy
A Bride for the Island Prince	Rebecca Winters
Pregnant with the Prince's Child	Raye Morgan
The Nanny and the Boss's Twins	Barbara McMahon
Once a Cowboy...	Patricia Thayer
Mr Right at the Wrong Time	Nikki Logan
When Chocolate Is Not Enough...	Nina Harrington
Sydney Harbour Hospital: Luca's Bad Girl	Amy Andrews
Falling for the Sheikh She Shouldn't	Fiona McArthur

HISTORICAL

Untamed Rogue, Scandalous Mistress	Bronwyn Scott
Honourable Doctor, Improper Arrangement	Mary Nichols
The Earl Plays With Fire	Isabelle Goddard
His Border Bride	Blythe Gifford

MEDICAL

Dr Cinderella's Midnight Fling	Kate Hardy
Brought Together by Baby	Margaret McDonagh
The Firebrand Who Unlocked His Heart	Anne Fraser
One Month to Become a Mum	Louisa George

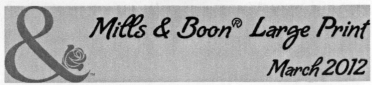

Mills & Boon® Large Print
March 2012

ROMANCE

The Power of Vasilii	Penny Jordan
The Real Rio D'Aquila	Sandra Marton
A Shameful Consequence	Carol Marinelli
A Dangerous Infatuation	Chantelle Shaw
How a Cowboy Stole Her Heart	Donna Alward
Tall, Dark, Texas Ranger	Patricia Thayer
The Boy is Back in Town	Nina Harrington
Just An Ordinary Girl?	Jackie Braun

HISTORICAL

The Lady Gambles	Carole Mortimer
Lady Rosabella's Ruse	Ann Lethbridge
The Viscount's Scandalous Return	Anne Ashley
The Viking's Touch	Joanna Fulford

MEDICAL

Cort Mason – Dr Delectable	Carol Marinelli
Survival Guide to Dating Your Boss	Fiona McArthur
Return of the Maverick	Sue MacKay
It Started with a Pregnancy	Scarlet Wilson
Italian Doctor, No Strings Attached	Kate Hardy
Miracle Times Two	Josie Metcalfe

McL